W9-BTK-038

Girl of the Shining Mountains

Girl of the Shining Mountains

SACAGAWEA'S STORY

PETER & CONNIE ROOP

HYPERION BOOKS FOR CHILDREN
NEW YORK

Printed in the United States of America.

First Edition

2 3 4 5 6 7 8 9 10

The text for this book is set in Adobe Garamond 13/17.

Library of Congress Cataloging-in-Publication Data

Roop, Peter.

Girl of the shining mountains: Sacagawea's story/Peter and Connie Roop—1st ed.

p.   cm.

Summary: Sacagawea describes how, at the age of sixteen, she becomes part of the Lewis and Clark expedition and serves as their interpreter and guide, surviving many dangerous adventures on their trek through the wilderness.

ISBN: 0-7868-0492-0.—0-7868-2422-0 (lib. bdg.)

1. Sacagawea, 1786–1884—Juvenile fiction. 2. Lewis and Clark Expedition (1804–1806)—Juvenile fiction. [1. Sacagawea, 1786–1884—Fiction. 2. Lewis and Clark Expedition (1804–1806)—Fiction. 3. Shoshoni Indians—Fiction. 4. Indians of North America—Fiction.]

I. Roop, Connie. II. Title.

PZ7.R6723Gi 1999   [Fic]—dc21   99-24227

*For Sterling and Heidi
as they set forth on life's journey.*

Girl of the Shining Mountains

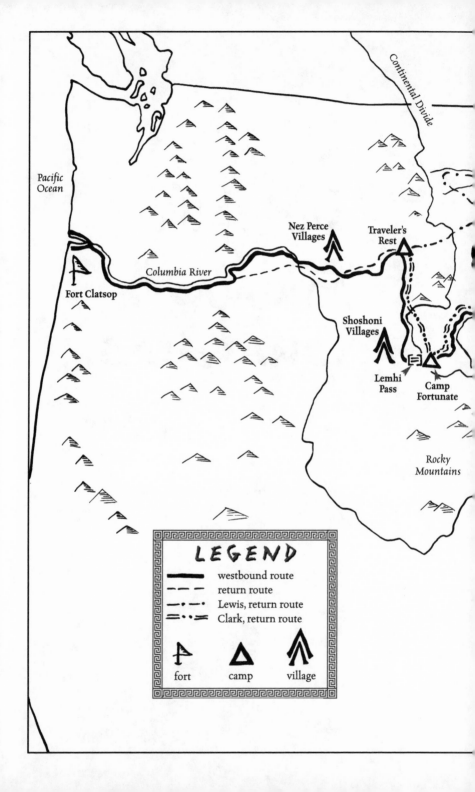

Sacagawea's Journey

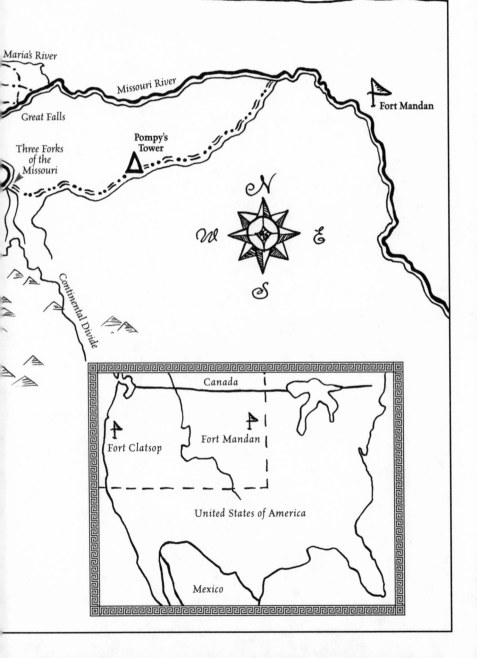

"Mama, tell me about your journey to the great salt lake, the Pacific Ocean."

"Pomp, your father can tell the story to you."

Charbonneau grunted. "No, my wife. You must tell the story. I am a trader, not a teller of tales. In any case, I do not need to hear it. I was there myself. I know all that happened." Charbonneau crossed to the bow of the flat-boat and lit his pipe.

"Mama. Please," Pomp begged. "I wish to hear your story before we reach Saint Louis." He pronounced it "San Louiee" like his French father did.

A flock of geese winged its way south before his mother answered.

"I will tell my story so when you are with Captain Clark you will not pester him with too many questions. He will think you are a mosquito buzzing in his ear."

She sighed. Where did the story truly begin? she wondered. When she was born Shoshoni, one of The People, in the Shining Mountains? Or when she was captured by her

1

tribe's enemies, the Hidatsa? Or when her husband, Charbonneau, won her as a gambling prize?

Did the story begin when Pomp was born one bitterly cold night in Isha-Mea'a, *the Coyote Moon?* Or when she first met Captain Lewis and Captain Clark in their winter fort along the banks of the Missouri? Did it begin when she and Charbonneau joined the captains on their journey to the western sea?

So many beginnings.

Where will my story end? she wondered.

She pulled her buffalo robe around her shoulders and began.

chapter

2

Long ago, before you were born, I lived with my family far to the west, toward the home of the setting sun. Your grandfather, my father, Strong Arm, was chief of our band of The People, the Shoshoni. He led us from our summer lodges to our winter home in the meadows of the Shining Mountains. He guided our men on buffalo hunts. He taught my brother, Cameahwait, to train wild horses. He showed him how to fish with a bone hook and to hunt with bow and arrows. He instructed him on the ways a warrior leads his people in peace and in war.

My mother, Bright Morning, was your grandmother. She taught me and my sisters, Quaking Leaf and Tall Grass, how to dig for roots and gather seeds and nuts. She showed us which berries were poisonous and which filled your belly. Her skilled fingers danced as they wove grass baskets and sewed buffalo skins for clothes and lodges. She taught us how to trap rabbits and make their furs into cloaks. From her, we learned to tan skins and chew them to make them as soft as goose down. Over her fire we dried meat and made stews. All these things a Shoshoni woman must know.

The winter of my eleventh circle of seasons was long. Our bellies ached from emptiness. The men hunted deer, elk, and buffalo. They killed few. Some of the very old and very young died before the buds opened on the trees.

When at last the warm winds of *Baduaa-Mea'a*, the Melting Moon, drove the ice from the rivers and the snow from the earth, The People were pleased. We raided the underground nests of mice for wild artichokes and nuts. We plucked green grass shoots and dug yampas roots to flavor the stews of elk meat Strong Arm and Cameahwait brought to our lodge.

As *Bu'Hisea-Mea'a*, the Budding Moon, grew round, we packed our lodges and moved down from our winter meadow to where the three rivers meet and become one. Look about you, son, for those three rivers join to make the beginnings of the Missouri, although I did not know that at the time. And just as the geese, ducks, and cranes return each spring from their winter homes, so do the buffalo. It was then we moved down from the mountains to meet them.

Our men prepared their horses and weapons for the spring buffalo hunt. The night before the hunt we danced and called to the buffalo. Our medicine man prayed to the Great Spirit for a good hunt. I gossiped with my friend Antelope, teasing her about a boy she liked. She teased me, too, about White Bear, who I was to marry. My father had gifted ten fine horses to White Bear's father for the honor.

"But you married Papa instead," Pomp interrupted.

"Yes, I did," she replied. *Although I had no choice either time, she thought.*

As the fire flickered in our lodge, Strong Arm taught Cameahwait the words to offer to the buffalo's spirit as he took its life. This was Cameahwait's first buffalo hunt with the men. He was so proud, your uncle. That night he slept with his best spear by his side. My sisters and I could hardly wait for him to make his first kill so we could fashion new moccasins for him from the skin. I had saved porcupine quills and dyed them yellow and red, his favorite colors, for this occasion.

An owl called, "WHOOOO WHOOOO," as I fell asleep.

Our hunters left at dawn, galloping to the east. Cameahwait rode tall beside our father. I remember thinking he will be a good chief someday, just like Strong Arm. The old men, women, and children stayed behind.

I went with Mama and my sisters, Quaking Leaf and Tall Grass, to collect yampas, the wild carrots you love so much. Antelope and her mother and aunts joined us. I remember the sun warm on my back and the jays chasing one another. Redheaded tanagers flitted through the trees, searching for insects. Squirrels scolded us.

Antelope and I, following a swarm of bees, wandered from the group. The bees led us to their honey tree, and we climbed to their hole to see how large the comb was.

High in the tree we looked at the world spreading below us. The three rivers wound together like braids. The towering mountains held us as if in a cup as round as one of Bright Morning's grass baskets.

Antelope saw the hunters' dust first.

"Look," she cried. "The men return. I hope our fathers killed many buffalo."

"I hope Cameahwait made his kill, too," I said.

As they got closer the galloping horses puzzled me. Through the dust and distance, they did not appear to be our spotted-rump horses.

I grabbed Antelope's arm. "Those are not our hunters. They are warriors of another tribe."

". . . Aiieee . . ." she yelled, and climbed down. She bounded like the antelope for which she is named to warn The People. I followed, reaching our families just as the war party burst through the trees.

From their clothes and weapons I knew them to be our hated enemies, the Hidatsa.

We scattered like seeds from a pod, just as we had been taught. This way we would be harder to capture. Or kill.

". . . Mama! . . ." I cried as a warrior galloped behind her. He swung his club. I willed my eyes to close. But I could not stop my ears from hearing a sound like a pumpkin being smashed.

I wanted to run to her, but the warrior turned his black gaze upon me. My heart aching, I plunged into the bushes, trying to escape. I ran like a rabbit fleeing a swooping hawk. Shouts and screams trailed me.

Someone crashed through the brush near me. I stole a glance. Antelope!

Our eyes met, but we said not a word. She waved for me to follow. I dodged in her direction, hoping to outrun my pursuer. Antelope was as fast as her name. If I could keep up with her, I might escape.

An arrow buzzed past my ear like an angry hornet. My lungs burned, but still we ran.

Ahead, water rushed around rocks. Once across the river we would be safe, I hoped. Antelope jumped from rock to rock like a fish leaping from the water. I was a few steps behind when I slipped and crashed into the water. My hair was yanked and I was pulled up. A knife flashed before my eyes. I was to be scalped!

All at once a whirlwind burst from the forest. Screaming like a panther, Antelope flew at my attacker. She knocked the knife from his hand and dug her fingers into his eyes. My world went black as my head cracked against a rock.

chapter 3

She shivered.

"Are you cold, Mama?" the little boy asked.

"No, but the memory of those days chills me still. Yet it does my heart good to share my story with you. Talking about your grandparents makes their memories bring warmth to my heart."

When I awoke, I found myself strapped over the back of a horse. My head hurt and my eyes could not see clearly. Slowly my eyes focused. I looked behind to see Antelope tied to a horse, too. Her eyes blazed with a fire I had never seen before. Even though it hurt, I turned my head to the front. As if my thoughts were his, our captor looked at us. A grin creased his face and he grunted at me. I shut my eyes, only to hear him laugh.

I struggled to free my hands from the buckskin ropes tying them, but I could not break or loosen them. Each time I looked back at Antelope she still had that same fierce fire burning in her eyes.

All day we bounced on those scrawny Hidatsa horses. Strong Arm would not even give such a poor horse to a child. The People's horses were well fed and strong. My eyes stung when I thought of Strong Arm. Was he alive? Had Cameahwait fallen beneath a Hidatsa club? My tears flowed, for I thought of my beautiful mother lying dead on the cold ground. Never again would she weave grass baskets or tell star stories or cradle me when I was with fever. I prayed to the Great Spirit that some of The People yet lived, so they could bury her body deep away from wolves and bears and properly send her spirit to the next world.

That evening we camped along a stream. My mouth burned. I licked my lips again and again. Finally our captor brought us food and water. He untied my arms. The numbness slowly went away. Then he tied my left arm to Antelope's right arm and he tied our feet so we could not escape. With our free arms we fed each other. Antelope's eyes glowed with hatred.

I looked around. Captured with us were two young girls and a boy. They were Bluestem, Wakes-At-Night, and Trout. Many times in our village I watched them play roll the hoop and chase the squirrel. Now, sobbing for their families, they huddled like frightened baby rabbits. My heart ached to reach out and comfort them, but the Hidatsa kept us apart. I counted the Hidatsa warriors. There were as many as the fingers on two hands. Five children against ten warriors.

We had no hope of escape.

As night fell, I watched the stars glide into the sky. An owl called, "WHOOOO WHOOO." Just the night before I had listened to an owl call as I lay in the tipi of my parents. Was it only the night before that my world had been at peace? That Strong Arm and Bright Morning chuckled over some shared joke? That Cameahwait slept with his spear, and my sisters and I planned our surprise for him?

Our captor tied my arms behind me again and bound me to Antelope.

I had fallen asleep when Antelope jabbed me awake.

"Do you have anything sharp?" she asked. "Like your scraping knife?"

"I left my pouch in our lodge," I whispered.

"I did, too," she answered. "I hoped you had yours."

We sat silently for many moments until only orange coals still burned in the campfire.

"I am going to escape," Antelope hissed.

"How?" I asked.

"I do not know yet. But I will never be a Hidatsa slave." Her harsh voice scraped against my ears. She pulled her arms. I had not known how strong she was. But each time she stretched against the ropes binding her, she hurt me. I bit my tongue so not a sound slipped from my lips.

Finally she gave up and said, "Tomorrow we will escape. Watch me. We must get away soon before we are so far from our lodges that we cannot find our way back."

Her words made sense to me. I told myself I would watch the trees and rocks and rivers and make them mine in my memory so I would never forget them and could use them to guide me home. Sleep came at last.

In the morning my arms ached, so that I could not raise them when our captor released them. My fingers felt as if bitten by the frost. We ate as we did the night before, one arm free, the other tied. Then we were bound to the horses again, this time sitting up.

All morning we rode. Warriors in front and behind. One warrior carried the little boy. The girls rode together. I could not see them, for they were in back, but I could hear their whimpering. I wished to hold them and tell them they would be fine. I would protect them like their mothers did.

Flies swarmed and bit us and we could do nothing but endure. Mosquitoes feasted upon us. I longed for bear grease to smear on my face, legs, and arms to keep them off.

My eyes wandered over the land, etching images into my mind. There was *Har-na-Hap-pap,* Beaverhead Rock, looming behind us. Here was a tree struck by lightning and split. I longed to dig a patch of yampas we passed. We traveled toward the rising sun and away from the setting sun. Even today I could find my way back home along our trail.

While my eyes filled with sights, my heart overflowed with sorrow. I tried to push thoughts of my family aside, to look for a way to escape.

That night the warriors fed us and tied us. Before I could be bound again to Antelope, I wiggled to the young children. My captor grunted and moved to break us apart. Another warrior said something to him and he let me stay. The girls and boy snuggled next to me. Like puppies we huddled together all night. My eyes met Antelope's across the fire. Her mouth smiled, but her eyes still flared.

When jays squawked at daybreak, my litter was with me. I looked for Antelope.

She was gone!

chapter 4

When the Hidatsa realized Antelope had escaped they began to search. Three went on foot and the rest on horseback.

Only one remained behind to guard us. He checked our bindings to make certain they were secure as he prepared our breakfast.

I hoped Antelope stayed free. Who knew what the warriors would do if they recaptured her? I shivered as I remembered my mother's death.

The little boy, Trout, looked up at me with his large eyes.

"Are you cold?" he asked.

"No," I told him. "I only hope Antelope gets back to The People."

Bluestem, the older girl said, "Wakes-At-Night complains her stomach hurts where a warrior hit her."

My mind flashed to my sisters, Quaking Leaf and Tall Grass. What had become of them? Would I ever know if they had lived or died? Certainly, they were not captives. Did they wonder and worry about me? I hugged Wakes-At-Night closer.

My thoughts ended with the return of the warriors. They said little, none of which I could understand. I did not speak the Hidatsa tongue at that time. But my heart soared. Antelope was not with them! Nor did her scalp hang from any belt. I asked the Great Spirit to guide her feet home to The People.

Would I ever see her again? I asked myself.

The days passed like the endless wind dancing across the plains. We rode. We walked. We ate. We slept. We rode. We followed a winding river. We galloped on a buffalo trail through a mountain gap. As a little girl your age I had crossed here with my family on a buffalo hunt. This trail led to the River of Yellow Stones. I tried to remember landmarks we passed. But each day it grew more difficult. I was tired. My legs and feet hurt. At a shallow place we forded the river. We were not bound any longer, but the warriors still kept a wary eye on me.

Wakes-At-Night worried me more than Trout and Bluestem. She would not talk, and we were thirteen suns from home. At night, while the others slept the sleep of the exhausted, she twitched like a dog with bad dreams. I held her close each night, and her movements awakened me often. I did not mind. The children were my family now. I was mother to them, tending their hurts, encouraging their hearts. I only wished someone could mother me, too.

Our long journey ended when we reached the Hidatsa village. The night before we arrived, the warriors chattered among themselves, smiling as they brushed their horses and cleaned their clothes.

Through hand signs my captor told me to wash the children and myself. He gave me a needle and thread to mend our torn clothes. I held the needle to the fire. It glittered like a silver ripple on water. Where did he get such a wonderful needle? It was steel, shaped like The People's bone needles but ever so much sharper and stronger. Now I know white traders like your father brought them.

Inside I smiled as I thought how much Bright Morning would have enjoyed using such a needle. My wounded heart ached for my mother, father, brother, and sisters. Yet with each passing day I felt a little more warmth return to my spirit. The three children of my new family helped.

That night I could have stolen away. The Hidatsa rarely watched us. What held me back? I thought I might be able to find my way home. I would not starve, for I knew where to dig for roots and how to snare rabbits. Bluestem, Trout, and Wakes-At-Night kept my feet from fleeing. Without me, what would happen to them?

Wakes-At-Night was especially wiggly until the moon set. Then, as if a breeze passed, she stilled. Her spirit left her frail body. She died in my arms. I turned my eyes to the stars, wishing farewell to her as she joined our ancestors. The stars blurred with my tears.

In the morning I buried her thin body. Trout and Bluestem helped me gather heavy stones from a stream to cover her so the wolves could not find her. I wanted to slash my hair as I knew a Shoshoni should. I would have done the same for my mother, for this is our way of honoring those who go before us. But I did not have my scraper or my knife. I mourned for my mother and my new sister in my heart.

chapter
5

When I first saw the Hidatsa village, I wondered where they lived. There were no buffalo-skin tipis or wickiups of brush. Only a wooden wall, inside of which were many dirt mounds. As we entered the wall, people popped out of the mounds like prairie dogs from their underground villages.

There were many more Hidatsa than The People in my Shoshoni band. They greeted the returning warriors with shouts of pleasure. We trailed behind, sad at such a joyful homecoming for them. I worried about our welcome.

My captor led me to a mound. A black hole opened into it. I jerked back, afraid to enter. The little ones held on to me until other Hidatsa yanked them away. I heard their wailing as I was shoved inside.

This lodge was bear-cave dark. It smelled of earth and smoke and people. A fire flickered in the center, its smoke rising to a hole in the roof. As my eyes adjusted to the light, I saw sleeping robes on platforms, weapons and shields hanging from the walls, buffalo-skin parfleches, and many other things I knew. There was also much unfamiliar to me, which I would soon learn.

A toothless old woman spoke with my captor. He grinned as he pushed me forward. She felt my arms and pried my mouth open to look at my teeth. She poked and prodded me like my father did when trading for a horse. She smiled and led me to her fire. She placed a buffalo-horn spoon in my hand and signed for me to stir a clay pot over the fire. I guessed she was my captor's mother.

Pointing at me, he said a word I did not know. *Sacagawea.*

With his arms flapping, he made the motion of a bird flying. I, who had enjoyed all birds from the swooping eagle to the darting hummingbird, from the booming prairie chicken to the trilling meadowlark, I, once free as the birds, was now a slave.

Perhaps my Hidatsa captor saw the longing in my heart to be as free as a hawk when he called me Sacagawea, for later I learned my new name meant Bird Woman.

My Hidatsa day was the same as any day with my people. Although I was a slave and could not wander freely, I worked just as I did before my capture. There were meals to cook, skins to scrape, clothes to mend and make, water to carry, wood to find, and dozens of other daily chores. It seemed my tasks were never done.

Like our Shoshoni men, the Hidatsa men were hunters and warriors. They protected us and brought us game. They trained the boys in skills of war and the hunt. They told stories, gambled, and played games.

The old woman who owned me was named Chokecherry Woman. She was nice to me in her own fashion, but many of her ways were strange. The strangest of all was the planting of seeds. The Shoshoni gathered seeds to make breads and flavor rabbit stews. The Hidatsa dug holes in mother earth and pushed the seeds into them.

One of my chores was to water a seed called maize. Never before had I seen this fat seed of many colors. My favorite seed color was blue. These seeds were as blue as the summer sky. To this day blue remains the color of my heart. Not only did the Hidatsa push these seeds into the earth, they ground them into a flour from which we made bread and other foods.

My greatest surprise that first year with the Hidatsa came when the seeds sprouted, but we were not allowed to eat the leaves. The plants grew and grew until they reached over my head. On the stalks grew plump pods with many new seeds. These we dried and separated into two piles. One pile was saved for planting the next spring when the geese returned. The other pile was for eating through the bitter winter when game was scarce.

The People always ate whatever seeds we could find

when we found them. Many were our winters of hunger.

Over time I came to tolerate my Hidatsa captors, although I never gave up my dream of returning to my family. Someday I would steal a knife and maize and escape. Someday, somehow, I would find my way home. *Someday, somehow.* I said these words over and over until they became a prayer for me.

I rarely saw Trout and Bluestem. They had been adopted by their captors and quickly became Hidatsa themselves. They dressed like them, played like them, laughed like them, even spoke like them. I promised myself I would remain Shoshoni. At night before I slept I told the story of my day to myself in our tongue, so I would never forget the words of The People.

I had hoped to take Trout and Bluestem with me when I escaped, but one traveling alone is safer than three together. I did not know even if they would wish to escape with me anymore. I dared not ask, in case they let my plans be known to their new families.

Chokecherry Woman taught me the language of the Hidatsa so I could better do the tasks she ordered me to do. She instructed me on how to mix buffalo meat, berries, and fat into pemmican. She watched me as I learned to grind maize and make bread with the flour. She laughed at my efforts to make pots of clay. I showed her how I could weave a basket from grass and smear the pitch from a pine tree to make it waterproof. She preferred her way and I mine. I learned to soften buffalo skins the Hidatsa way, but did it the Shoshoni way when she was not watching.

Chokecherry Woman also was looking for a husband for me. She often said, "A person without relatives is nothing." I hoped to remain nothing until I found my way home. Marrying White Bear would be a pleasure!

Chokecherry Woman wanted my husband to have many horses to give for me. At least, that is what she told me. Instead, after one circle of the seasons, she returned me to her son. He did not desire me for a wife. His heart was set on another girl, Cottonwood.

One day he was gambling with the white traders who lived in the village. My captor lost a bet on the shell game. To honor his debt he offered me to the winner, Charbonneau.

That is how I came to marry your father, Charbonneau, when I was only thirteen years old. And that is how you came into this world two years later.

When I lived with the Shoshoni, I had never seen a white man. In the Hidatsa village there were as many white men as the fingers on two hands. The Hidatsa were friendly to these traders and trappers, for they provided the tribe with steel knives, iron kettles, needles, blankets, gunpowder, axes, and other things we needed. For these goods, the Hidatsa traded the furs of the beaver, buffalo, bear, elk, and wolf.

I joined your father and his first wife in their small earth lodge. The first wife grew to be my friend, almost a second sister. Her name was Otter Woman. She, too, was one of The People and had been captured during a raid upon the Shoshoni, although she was not of my band. Together we lived well, for your father spoke the language of the Hidatsa and the Mandan who lived down the river from our village. In his trades, he was as stubborn as a Hidatsa woman, somehow always managing to make a pleasing bargain.

The Mandan lived much as the Hidatsa did, in earth lodges surrounded by fields of maize. They, too, hunted the buffalo and traded with the white men.

Never before had the Hidatsa or Mandan seen as many white men as followed Captain Lewis and Captain Clark. We knew they were traveling up the river. Our scouts had seen them days before they arrived near where the Knife River shares its water with the Missouri.

They reached us at the end of *Naa-Mea'a,* the moon when the deer rut. Already the Coldmaker had sent flurries of snow. We had harvested much maize and the men had brought in much meat, so we did not fear the long winter ahead. I was heavy with you, Pomp, and looked forward to when you would be born that winter.

I wished to see these white men, as I heard strange tales from those who met them. I did not believe any of these fantastic tales. One leader named Clark had hair as red as a sunset. A giant man called York had skin as black as a charcoaled log. A dog as big as a baby buffalo traveled with them and hunted for them. They had many guns and many things to trade with us. I wanted to see these wonders for myself.

My heart smiled, for I remembered my mother teasing me about my curiosity.

Why does the eagle have a white head?

Why does the cold wind blow from the north?

Why do geese flock together?

Why does a yampas root taste so good when boiled and bitter when not?

The captains had been sent by their chief, named Jefferson, to travel to where the sun sets in the great lake far to the west. When the geese returned they would continue their journey. My heart leaped when I heard this. They might travel to the land of the Shoshoni! Aieee! If only I could journey with them.

I begged your father to take me to see them. He learned from a trader Captain Lewis and Captain Clark were in need of an interpreter who could speak with the Indian tribes to the west. He hoped to be the interpreter and earn valuable trade goods.

One sunny day Otter Woman and I paddled your father in our round bullboat across the river to the white men's fort. The walls stood as tall as those surrounding the Hidatsa village. There was one opening with a gate. Each night the Indians inside left the fort and the gate was barred. The white men were friendly, yet they sought protection, too. They had troubles with the Sioux farther downstream and did not wish to be attacked by the Hidatsa and Mandan.

Your father talked for a long time with the captains. He told them he spoke French, Hidatsa, and the language of hand signs.

I stood behind him and let my eyes wander around the log room while they talked. I saw the big black dog. Captain Lewis called him Seaman. The dog was bigger than any I had ever seen before. He sniffed me and licked my hand and lay down at my feet. I petted him while the discussions continued. I looked for the man with skin the color of coal, but I did not see him.

All at once Papa grabbed my hand and pulled me to the front. I lowered my eyes before the captains. My heart fluttered and fear rippled through my skin. Clark, with hair the color of fire, gently put his hand under my chin and raised my face so I had to look at him.

He smiled and held his arms like he was rocking a baby. I ran my hand over my swollen belly and smiled back.

Then he spoke to a man who spoke to your father in the language of the French. Papa nodded and said, *"Oui! Oui!"* many times.

All of this was very strange to me as I understood not a word. I hoped my husband would get to go with the captains as he was determined to do so. Otter Woman and I could survive together without him for one circle of the seasons.

Later, my heart soared like the eagle, when your father explained to me that I was to go, too! The captains needed someone who spoke Shoshoni so they could trade for horses to cross the Shining Mountains.

At last I could return home and be with my true family again.

Otter Woman was angry she could not go, too. She broke a clay pot on purpose and spoiled our dinner that night. Your father scolded her and left to join the men gambling. Otter Woman and I did not speak. Our lodge crackled with energy.

I left and spent the night with Chokecherry Woman. She was pleased for me and we chattered about the journey until the stars faded from the sky and the sun rolled over the horizon.

I knew it would be hard to wait the five moons before the captains would leave. But I had a baby coming, and that filled my heart with as much pleasure as my desire to return to The People.

7

Your father and I wintered with Captain Lewis and Captain Clark in their fort. Unlike the Mandan and Hidatsa, we did not have to leave each night. Captain Lewis asked Papa many questions, always about what lay up the Missouri River.

He wished to know what tribes he might encounter. What animals he might see. What plants he might find. He desired to know how far away the thundering falls were. He wished to know all the rivers flowing into the Missouri and where they mixed their waters.

He asked your father to ask me many times where the Shoshoni lived. How many horses did they own? Would they sell horses to the expedition? Could I guide his men to the Shoshoni? I told him, "Yes, I could guide him to The People."

Yet even as I promised him, I questioned whether I could. My Hidatsa captors had not followed the Missouri River. They had followed the River of Yellow Stones. I believed if we drew near to the land of The

People, I would remember the trees and mountains. Each time he asked, a picture of *Har-na-Hap-pap*, Beaverhead Rock, formed in my mind. Yes, I could guide them to The People. Even if I did not succeed, I would be closer to home than I had been since my capture.

Each day my eyes filled with wonder at the activities of Captain Lewis and Captain Clark. They spent many days visiting the Mandan and Hidatsa villages. They asked many questions. Each night they wrote in leather-covered books of what they learned that day. Sometimes they drew pictures of animals and plants.

They collected buffalo robes, moccasins, parfleches, bows, and arrows from the Mandan and Hidatsa. They said they were for their chief, President Jefferson. He was a man of great curiosity and wished to know the people, plants, and animals of this land because all here was new to him.

Captain Lewis's dog, Seaman, became my companion when he was not with Captain Lewis. I enjoyed throwing sticks across the snow. He would chase after them as if they were ducks he was bringing to Captain Lewis.

Captain Clark had a slave named York. He was the man with the skin of charcoal. To me York seemed more of a companion than a slave. He helped Captain Clark with his tasks. He hunted. He joined in the songs and games the men played. He reminded me greatly of my brother, Cameahwait, with his strong laughter and his gentle strength.

Many Mandan and Hidatsa were in awe of York. To play tricks he would growl at the women to frighten them. The men tried to rub the black from his skin and were amazed when it stayed. With the children, York was tender. He made them toys of wood to play with and gave them rides on his broad back.

I was surprised Captain Clark would own another man, but many ways of the white men puzzled me. Yet, I, too, had been a slave and understood the far-away look York sometimes had in his eyes.

Their chief, Jefferson, wanted Captain Lewis and Captain Clark to be friends with every tribe they met. They were generous with gifts of beads, mirrors, needles, axes, and paints.

Forty men lived in the fort. Feeding them was hard work. To find enough meat the hunters had to brave the cold as well as the lurking Sioux. Captain Lewis hunted for a week and returned with fourteen elk and thirty-six deer. We ate well and he gifted much meat to the Mandan.

The Mandan and Hidatsa traded maize to the captains. They sent their hunters for buffalo, often inviting the captains to join them.

I remember the day Coldmaker's icy breath froze the Missouri. Fifteen men from the fort were hunting buffalo with Chief Shehek of the Mandan. They rode out early in the morning and returned late in the afternoon with many buffalo. Captain Clark himself killed five. We feasted that night, but saved meat to be smoked and jerked for the journey ahead.

Three men had returned with their feet badly frostbitten. I watched Captain Clark treat their injuries. His big hands were tender as he warmed the men's frozen toes. With hand signs I asked to help, and he let me. Many were the times when The People had frostbite. I knew what to do.

My favorite day all winter was the day called Christmas. The men awakened the captains by firing their guns and yelling. There was much cheering when Captain Lewis raised the flag of the Americans over the fort for the first time.

The men traded gifts with one another. Captain Clark gave me a belt of beads as blue as the summer sky. I wore them with pride, thinking how jealous my sisters, Quaking Leaf and Tall Grass, would be to see me wearing them. Not knowing about the gift trading, I had nothing to give in return. I was determined someday to give Captain Clark a special gift.

Monsieur Cruzatte, one of the captains' men, made much music on his violin. The men danced until their legs grew too tired to continue. Their celebration lasted long into the night.

My wonderment grew when seven days later, the captains, York, Cruzatte, and many men visited the

Indian villages, singing and dancing. The funny Frenchman Cruzatte even danced on his hands! Your father explained that this celebration was the white men's way of marking the beginning of a new circle of the moons. A new year had begun.

After this our Mandan friends held many nights dancing. They asked the buffalo to return so they could hunt them. The red men, white men, and black man moved to the music of turtle-shell rattles and buffalo-skin drums.

Gos-Mea'a, the Freezing Moon, the first moon of the new year, was long and cold. Snow flew through the air day and night. Our drinking water froze inside the cabin. The captains kept the men busy hunting, chopping wood, and repairing their boats, guns, and tools. The men were never idle.

Food became scarce for both the white men and the Indians. The Hidatsa women were able to get more trade goods for their maize than when Captain Lewis and Captain Clark first came. I know they kept baskets hidden so they would not starve and there would be maize to plant when the geese returned. One soldier named Shields made iron battle-axes, arrow points, and buffalo-hide scrapers to trade. He received eight baskets of maize for each thing he made. In this way, the captains kept hunger away from the fort.

While I watched and learned, I also felt you kicking inside me, Pomp. You twisted and turned day and night as if you could not wait to see the world yourself.

Finally the day came when I was to hold you for the first time and look into your black eyes. *Isha-Mea'a,* the Coyote Moon, shone upon your birth.

You were my first child, and your birth was difficult for me. Many long hours I labored to bring you into the world. Finally, to ease your birth, Captain Clark had me eat the crushed rattles of a snake.

Soon you were born!

I wrapped you in a rabbit-skin robe I had made for you and held you close. My heart flooded with love for you while my eyes flowed with tears wishing your grandmother, Bright Morning, was yet alive to hold you, too. If we were with the Shoshoni, my brother, Cameahwait, your uncle, would teach you how to hunt and fish, and to be the bravest of The People.

Now, because you are half Shoshoni and half French, you will learn the white man's ways with Captain Clark in Saint Louis. I think this is his way of thanking me for what I did for the captains and their men.

Yet we almost did not get to make the journey at all, for your father did a foolish thing. He told the captains he would not go with them if he had to do the duties of a soldier. Papa proudly exclaimed he was an interpreter and would serve only as such.

The captains ordered him to leave the fort and take us with him. My heart was split. One half was angry at your father, for he had spoiled my chance of returning home. The other half knew I must obey my husband.

Taking my few possessions, wearing my blue-bead belt, and carrying you, I trailed behind Papa as we left the fort.

Back in our cold earthen lodge I told your father what I thought. I had nothing to lose. Even if he sent me from our lodge, I had you for my family. Somehow, some way, I would find my way back to The People.

He raised his hand to hit me. I stood as still as a lodge pole. I would take my beating. But you cried, and he stormed from the lodge.

Papa fumed and fretted. I refused to speak to him. I served him food and gathered wood. I did my chores. He threatened to beat me.

I knew he desired to journey with Captain Lewis and Captain Clark. He wanted their pay. Yet, even in his anger, he knew I was important, too. Without me, the white men might not find the Shoshoni and be able to trade for horses.

Seven suns passed before your father returned to the fort. He begged to join the captains. He promised he would do all of his duties. He prayed to his god they would take him back. I asked the Great Spirit that this would be so, and I could return to my people. After much talk, the captains agreed and let Papa join them again.

My heart soared like an eagle over Beaverhead

Rock once more. When the geese returned, we would begin our journey back to The People. My only worry was to convince Papa that we should remain with the Shoshoni. I would tell him he would be an important man and become a powerful trader.

chapter 8

When you were two moons old in *Yu'a Mea'a,* the Warming Moon, I took you outside to watch the swans and geese return. They flew overhead, searching for food and open water. The river was still frozen except where the men chopped their big boat free of the ice. You smiled as I held you high. You heard geese honking for the first time.

Coldmaker was loosening his icy grip. Soon the ice would be off the river and we would travel west toward the Shining Mountains.

Captain Clark, for some reason I do not understand, began calling me Janey.

"Like he called me Pomp, although Papa calls me Jean Baptiste?" Pomp queried.

"Yes," Sacagawea answered. "He gave you a second name as he did me. He explained to Monsieur Jessaume, another interpreter like Papa, that Pomp meant a great leader. Monsieur Jessaume said it in French to Papa who told me in Hidatsa. Pomp was the first American word I learned to speak. Captain Clark later named a tall rock

by the River of Yellow Stones Pompy's Tower in your honor."

This naming of things is something I did not understand when I was first with the captains. They gave new names to the land, changing the names for which they were known by the tribes. Every river they saw, they gave it a white man's name. Every plant or animal or rock they did not know they named and collected it like the Shoshoni collect seeds.

"But why did he call you Janey?" Pomp asked, unable to hold back.

"Maybe he could not fit his tongue around Sacagawea. Or maybe I reminded him of a Janey faraway at his own home. Many nights I wondered about the captains and their men all traveling far from family and friends to reach the salt water they called the ocean. They knew foes might await them or hunger find them or accident befall them. Yet they were determined to follow their dream to reach the great salt lake."

I, too, was determined to follow my dream up the river to my home with The People. But we had to wait for the ice to leave the river.

While we waited I spent many hours with Captain Lewis as he struggled to write the Hidatsa tongue on his special papers. These he would send to President Jefferson in the spring.

First I would say a word, like buffalo or cottonwood or sun, in Hidatsa. Then your father would say it in French to Monsieur Jessaume. He would then say the word in the language of the Americans. Each time I would try to repeat the word to myself. Many times I wished to laugh because the words sounded so funny on my tongue. Captain Lewis was too serious with his work, and so I bundled my laughter inside until I could whisper the words to you, Pomp.

During this time Captain Clark drew a map of the Missouri. Every Indian he questioned, he asked, What lay upstream? Which rivers flowed into the Missouri? From which direction did they flow? How far away were the Shining Mountains? He asked and asked and asked, even though many told him different things. The Mandan and Hidatsa drew their own maps in the dust as they explained to him what they knew of the river.

On special paper, like Captain Lewis, he wrote these things down. Later, when he had balanced a Hidatsa's information against a Minnetree's, against an Akikara's, then he put it on his map. He showed it to me many times and asked me in hand signs where the Shoshoni lived and how far it was across the Shining Mountains to the salt lake. I so wished I could speak his tongue. That way our words would carry their true meanings.

When I was your age, Pomp, I had heard of the great lake where the water tastes like salt. No one I knew had ever been there. No one the captains met had either. Yet they told of another river, like the Missouri, which flowed not toward the rising sun but toward the setting sun. This river the captains would find for Jefferson, their chief.

Many times I hoped that which the Indians told the captains was true, for it meant they would continue their journey at least as far as The People. After that, I did not care, for I only wanted to be with my family again.

The fort bustled like a village of ants now that the weather was warmer. The men chopped the boats free from the ice and repaired them. In the Indian fashion, they made canoes from great cottonwood trees, six in all.

I jerked much buffalo meat to eat as we traveled. I made many moccasins from elk hide and taught York how to make them, too. His large fingers soon learned how to make small stitches without drawing blood. Many times I thought he is like one of The People. I carefully repaired Papa's tipi of buffalo skin that would be our home until we reached The People again.

The men prepared their large keelboat to carry things to Saint Louis and then to Washington, where Jefferson lived. I puzzled about what they sent him. Did they not have these things in Washington? I wondered. They packed plants and seeds they had gathered, everything from the purple coneflower to watercress. They sent rocks of all shapes and sizes: heavy ones, light ones, round ones, and smooth ones. Skeletons of the fleet antelope were carefully wrapped along with those of mice, deer, and insects. Animal skins were dried and cleaned: elk, mule deer, beaver, buffalo, and smaller animals. Included in a special bundle was a large buffalo skin decorated with pictures of a battle between the Minnetree and the Mandan.

Four magpies squawked in their wooden cages. One of my tasks was to feed them as well as the prairie dog and prairie hen in their cages. Jefferson, their chief, must indeed be a very curious man.

What was his village like, I wondered?

What animals lived there?

What plants did the women dig and cook?

My mind puzzled over these things as I worked.

All the while, Captain Lewis wrote letters. Captain Clark drew his map. The map and letters were carefully wrapped and packed.

Thus it was late one afternoon in *Badua'a-Mea'a*, the Melting Moon, or April, as the captains called it, that the loaded keelboat pushed off into the Missouri current and floated downstream just as we do now.

Before I stepped into the white pirogue in which your father and I were to ride, Otter Woman came to me. I carried you then in a robe tied across my chest. Otter Woman held out to me the cradleboard she had been making for her firstborn. It was cottonwood and decorated with a rainbow of dyed porcupine quills.

Many times I had gazed at it in our lodge as she worked on it. I placed you in the cradleboard and climbed in the pirogue.

My eyes blurred with tears as we pushed away from shore. I knew I would never see Otter Woman again. She had been my only friend, ever since Antelope escaped. Our wet eyes and wide smiles met as we parted.

The men dug their paddles into the churning, brown water. The canoes and pirogues moved slowly against the current.

9

At first I was uncomfortable in the pirogue. I sat still, not daring to shift my weight even as you pulled down my shoulders. I was used to our round bullboats, which floated like big bowls and were easily paddled. Bullboats skimmed across the water, not slicing it like canoes did.

Captain Clark commanded the water craft while Captain Lewis walked the shore. Seaman barked and chased rabbits as he followed his master.

We did not travel far that first day. I was disappointed, for I wished to cover much distance and be closer to home. At sunset we made camp. With York's help, I put up the tipi, which we shared with the captains and Monsieur Drouillard, a most excellent hunter and interpreter. York laughed his great booming laugh as he struggled with the poles. Each time he stood them up, they fell, until I showed the Shoshoni way of making them stand together and support one another. York and I became good at setting up the tipi when we made camp and taking it down when we traveled again. This was one of the many tasks we came to share.

We unrolled our buffalo robes and slept. It was difficult for me to find sleep, for I was eager to be on our journey. In my mind's eye I could see returning to my village. I would hold you up so my friends and family could see the new Shoshoni warrior I was bringing home. As the fire died out I closed my eyes. I knew I would need my strength to make such a journey, to do my tasks, and to care for you.

That evening Captain Lewis was happier than I had ever seen him. At times he seemed to disappear faraway into his own thoughts as if he were already crossing the Shining Mountains. At this first camp, he was like a child, like you are, Pomp, with your willow whistle. He talked and laughed with the men resting around the fires. By candlelight he wrote in his book for a long time, glancing up at us and smiling. Even though he had walked many miles that day, he, too, tossed and turned in his buffalo robe as if he could not wait for day to break so we could be on the trail again. He made me think of a dark coal blown into a bright flame.

Outside Seaman guarded the entrance flap to the tipi, against what I knew not. Yet he did as Captain Lewis ordered him. From his expression I could tell Captain Lewis feared someone might steal Seaman, as he was a wonder to all who met him. He was very friendly to me, and he loved it when you pulled his floppy ears. He licked your face to make you giggle. But I get ahead of my story.

The next morning the wind blew hard against us. The men paddled with all of their strength, but the wind often proved stronger. Captain Clark urged the men on as a Shoshoni warrior urges on his horse in battle. Soon one of the canoes fell far behind. We pulled into shore, and Captain Clark returned to find the canoe full of water. Everything in it was wet.

The sun shone warm and, out of the grasping fingers of the wind, the men spread the wet things out to dry. Robes, blankets, gunpowder, rifles, and many other items dried while we ate a meal of buffalo jerky and water.

That evening we camped on an island in the river. A Mandan man and his woman visited us. The woman wished to travel with us as she was a friend of the young soldiers. The captains refused to let her. I was saddened, as I had hoped to have another woman for company. Yet I had you, Pomp, to keep me busy as well as my other chores.

We passed many villages. The people flocked like ducks to the river to see us. Captain Clark said farewell to his friend Black Cat, chief of the Mandan. Black Cat gave him a beautiful pair of moccasins, which he put on immediately to show his appreciation. Many times I repaired the soles of Captain Clark's moccasins on our journey, especially when he stepped on the sharp barbs of the prickly pear cactus.

We traveled fast the following day, but not so fast as the great flocks of geese, which swam up the river. A gentle breeze pushed us. The men raised the sails on the pirogues and we flew like swans. The maples, elms, and cottonwoods had begun to bloom, their tiny green leaves reminding me of Otter Woman.

Now she was alone. She would have to plant the maize we saved from the last harvest by herself. In my heart I wished her happiness, for I was happy, too. I had a baby and I was closer to my home. My only worry was if your father would allow us to stay with my people. I wondered, too, if he would stay with them over the next winter or continue on with the captains to the ocean. I knew I would remain.

That evening I proved my usefulness to the captains. I knew the men's bellies ached from eating only jerked meat each day, for the hunters had poor luck in killing game. They needed much meat to eat to keep up their strength as they paddled against the spring current. After York and I set up the tipi, I gathered dry driftwood for the fire we would have in the lodge that night. Although the buds were out and the grass was greening and the first flowers blooming, the night air still chilled, even when we were wrapped in our robes.

I picked up an armload of sticks and stopped, for I remembered how the people gathered wild artichokes each spring. I leaned you in your cradleboard against a cottonwood. I took a sharp stick and began digging in the burrows of the gophers. I poked my stick into the ground until I felt it hit an artichoke root. Then I dug down, uncovering the gopher's hoard of these delicious plants. I soon gathered many roots and their stems as well. The roots were about the size of a man's finger. These I took to the captains, who were pleased with them.

I cooked the roots the Shoshoni way and they ate them with pleasure. Captain Clark signed they reminded him of a plant he was familiar with. From that day I gathered these and other roots, nuts, and berries to help feed the hungry men.

Every morning we rose before the sun and traveled early so as to be ahead of the wind. Some days it blew gentle. Other days it was as if a mighty hand was trying to keep us from making our way. Each day we saw more geese, swans, cranes, and ducks. The men hunted antelope, buffalo, and elk, sometimes with success, sometimes not.

One morning Captain Clark decided to walk the shores, and Captain Lewis took command of the canoes. Captain Clark invited me to join him, and together we walked many miles with you, Pomp, bouncing on my back. When we rested, Captain Clark held you, signing he had small relatives, too, and you made him think of his own family far away. I wondered if he had a wife, but did not have the words or the courage to ask.

We saw many antelope feeding on the prairie but could not get close enough to kill any. But mosquitoes we did kill. The warm weather brought them out like hungry wolves feeding on an injured buffalo. I smeared bear grease on your hands and face to keep them away.

We saw great clouds of black smoke rising to the sky. At first, I thought it was the Minnetree burning the prairie to encourage the new grass to grow stronger and to bring back more buffalo for their hunters. We discovered it was a river bluff burning. A long seam of black rock smoldered and flamed. Captain Clark was excited about this, and he wrote about it in his journal book. Each time we found the black rocks, burning or not, the captains wrote about it. Their chief, Jefferson, must need to know of this wonder, too.

One day three French trappers joined us. Your papa was excited and talked with them much about their trapping. These things he shared with the captains, who were much pleased to learn so many beaver lived along the Missouri. The trappers had twelve beaver skins and indicated there were many more. The pelts were winter-thick and very soft. The men shared the beaver tails. I made a stew of them with my day's roots so each man got a piece of fat, tender beaver meat.

Many springs trickled into the river, but we could

not drink from them. They smelled like old geese eggs that had not hatched. Captain Lewis tasted several of them and made a face like he had eaten something bitter. Captain Clark laughed at him and said something to him in their tongue that I did not understand. Captain Lewis laughed, too. They were both chiefs of our traveling tribe, sharing their command equally. The power of their friendship was as brilliant as the moon on a clear, cold night.

We saw three cranes winging their way west along the river bottoms. I truly loved these tall white birds with their black wing tips. Their calls echoed over the river like the distant whooping of hunters jubilant after a successful hunt.

This day we ate better, for the man called Drouillard killed a deer. We ate venison steaks, beaver tails, two geese Captain Lewis shot, with biscuits cooked by Papa. I had never known him to cook, as Otter Woman and I did this duty in the Hidatsa village. Your father proved to be an excellent cook and often helped me make meals. This skill helped the captains remain pleased with him, because many other times he did foolish things that greatly angered them.

"What foolish things did Papa do?" Pomp interrupted. He looked at his father standing in the bow talking with another traveler. His large hands waved in the air as he told a story. The other man threw back his head and laughed.

"Did he say funny things like he does to me?" Pomp asked.

Sacagawea pulled Pomp close. "No, he did something that endangered you, something I can never forget."

"What was that?"

"Tomorrow, I will tell you. I am tired now and we must prepare for sleep."

"Please, Mama, please tell me tonight," he begged.

"We have many days still to travel to Saint Louis. I cannot tell you the entire story in just one," Sacagawea explained.

Pomp puckered his lips in a pout, but did not argue anymore.

"Bon soir, *Mama*," he whispered.

Sacagawea smiled at him and said, "Bon soir, *my French Shoshoni*."

10

I n the morning Sacagawea waited until her husband was out of earshot before continuing her story. Pomp was impatient for her to begin, but she hushed him and hugged him. A strong wind ruffled his hair as it did the waves upon the water.

"I will miss you while you live with Captain Clark," she said. "We have done much together, you and I."

"But I will learn to make words on paper like Captain Clark does. And draw maps like he does. And be friends with all the tribes like he is."

"And you will pester him each day for a story like you do me." Sacagawea sighed. "I did the same with my father. He and his father before him and his father before him told all the Shoshoni stories from the time The People first came on earth. He told how Coyote opened the grass basket that Wolf had given him to protect and how The First People escaped onto earth. And he told how Coapiccan the Giant caught unsuspecting people with a hooked branch and placed them in his basket to eat."

"But, Mama, I know those stories. You have told them

to me since I was a baby. Now tell me the foolish thing Papa did."

Sacagawea took a deep breath and began.

I have told you how the wind was sometimes our friend, sometimes our foe. This wind today reminds me of the wind that day. My eyes were often aimed at the sky, watching the birds flying north. Never before had I seen so many birds. I wondered at this. Maybe we did not have so many birds in the mountains, as there was not enough room for them. Or down in the villages there were too many people and hunters, so the birds shied away. Here we were the only people, and the birds were in a hurry to feed and fly north to make their summer homes. Just as the Shoshoni move from their winter lodges to their summer lodges, so must the cranes, swans, geese, and ducks.

The captains, too, enjoyed the birds. They watched them and wrote about them in their books. I told them the Shoshoni and Hidatsa names for each one.

This day the wind blew very strong in our direction and was our friend. Captain Lewis walked the shore. We were in the white pirogue. The men raised the sails and we moved swiftly up the river, even though there were waves splashing over the sides.

Our boat was heavily loaded, for the captains felt it was the safest and strongest of the canoes. They had placed the bundles of presents for the Indians we would meet. I sat on their boxes of instruments with you in your cradleboard strapped to my back. The captains wrapped their books and other important papers. These were in buckskins bundled in front of me. There were other boxes of medicines, food, cans of gunpowder, the needle that always points to the star of the north, and many other things they wanted to keep safe.

Three men who could not swim rode with us that day. The wind blew hard all morning and into the afternoon. We did not stop for dinner as we were making such good progress. Like Captain Lewis, I wished to hurry to the Shining Mountains as fast as we could travel. Missing a meal meant nothing if I got home sooner.

We were far out onto the river where it is very wide. The wind made the waves tumble upon us, soaking us with their spray. Still we sailed onward. On the distant shore I saw Captain Lewis with Seaman.

Papa was steering the pirogue when a sudden gust of wind hit us, yanking the sail ropes from the men's hands. The sail flapped like a wounded goose.

The boat swerved. The wind smacked us on the side. Papa yelled and let go of the steering oar. Drouillard drew his pistol and threatened to shoot Papa if he did not grab the steering oar.

Water flooded into the boat, rapidly filling it. Drouillard shouted at Papa and pushed him out of the way. He grasped the steering oar and turned the boat so the water stopped coming in. But it was too late. Boxes and bundles floated out of the boat.

I was in the back. As the boxes and bundles drifted toward me, I grabbed as many as I could. I held as many as I could. You were crying. Papa was praying to his Great Spirit to save him. My fingers ached, but I did not want to lose anything. Only if we sank would I release them and swim with you to the shore.

On shore Captain Lewis shouted. Seaman barked frantically.

One man awoke as if from a dream, and he began snatching things. The other canoes behind us plucked boxes out of the water.

Drouillard sailed us to shore where Captain Lewis waited. He had his coat off, for he was ready to plunge into the river to aid us.

His angry face was as red as Captain Clark's hair. He shouted at your father, who hung his head in shame. I watched Papa's fists clench and unclench. He was angry, too, but dared not argue with Captain Lewis. I hoped he would not argue, for if he did and the captains wished to have him leave the company, we must leave, too.

Captain Lewis smiled at me, and made signs to show how he was pleased with me. I thought it was nothing, for all I did was hold on to some packages. Only if you, Pomp, were in danger would I have let them go.

That evening, as an apology for his mistake, Papa fixed a special meal of *boudin blanc*. He made this sausage of buffalo meat and fried it in bear oil until it was crispy brown and filled the camp with its delicious smell. The men, who enjoyed buffalo meat, especially liked Papa's *boudin blanc*. They begged him to make it whenever he could.

And he did, for he wished to prove to the captains that, even if he was not a good waterman, he was worth keeping on the journey. I helped him make the sausages as I, too, wished to finish my journey.

I only hoped Captain Lewis would not let him steer the boat again.

"Did he?" Pomp asked.

"No," Sacagawea answered. "But Papa did cook boudin blanc *many, many times."*

11

That evening around the fires there was talk about white bears. Captain Clark called them grizzly bears, and he greatly wanted to hunt one.

We were camped on a flat area above the river. All along the shore were white bear tracks. The bears had been feeding on buffalo, which had died falling through the winter ice. Their carcasses lay in shallow water, and the bears feasted on them.

The captains and the men were excited about hunting a white bear. At Fort Mandan they had heard stories of hunters attacking a bear only to become the hunted themselves when the bear charged them. I told Papa how The People prepared to hunt a white bear. We never hunted him alone. Eight or ten warriors with quivers full of arrows and strong bows went to battle the bears.

The night before a hunt the men painted themselves as if going to fight a human enemy. To kill a white bear brought great honor to one's family. Your uncle, Cameahwait, wished to kill one as your grandfather, Strong Arm, had done. But he needed to be much more skilled with his bow. Many times men who went to hunt the white bear did not return to their families. The bears won more battles than they lost.

But the captains and men were eager to match their weapons against the claws and teeth of the white bear. I feared for them, knowing what I knew about the bear's power and strength.

Captain Clark shot an elk and the sound of his firing brought two white bears from their feeding. The bears rumbled up the opposite bank of the river and disappeared. The distance was too far for a gunshot, and the men laughed at the frightened bears. I did not laugh, for I remembered Basking Turtle, who did not return from a white bear hunt.

The men looked for white bears, but we saw no more for many days. We did see eagles, swans, geese, ducks, cranes, and prairie grouse. The sky and river were flooded with birds. Our ears filled with their cries and calls. There were beaver, elk, deer, antelope, buffalo, and villages of prairie dogs. The elk and buffalo were too lean from the hard winter to make much of a meal. With my roots and a little meat and bone marrow, I helped fill the men's empty bellies.

Many days I would walk the shore with either Captain Lewis or Captain Clark, and with you on my back. These were the days when the wind was blowing strong in our faces and the men had a hard time moving the canoes against the wind and the current. I walked to make the load lighter. Sometimes we walked all day. At other times we walked and collected roots. You and I would wait for the canoes to come up the river and join us. I would feed you, play with you, talk to you in Shoshoni, and let you lie on your back and watch the clouds run across the sky.

Every night one or both of the captains wrote about our day in his book. The men used this time to dry wet things and make repairs. They kept their eyes on the lookout for a white bear. Finding one seemed like a game to them.

Coldmaker was not finished with his season. Some mornings ice glistened on the river's edge and frost sparkled on the canoes. Each day the sun climbed higher and the captains pushed toward the mountains.

The river ran high, carrying broken trees, logs, drowned buffalo, and elk. The men dodged these things as best they could. Each canoe carried a long pole to push objects out of the way if they came too close.

One day we cut across the river to take advantage of the slow current near the shore. We were strung out in a line like baby ducks following their mother. Even by the shore the current was strong. I heard the earth rip and watched a giant cottonwood begin to tip over. The earth bank slid into the river, making tall waves, which rocked the canoes, splashing water into them.

One canoe, the nearest to the collapsing bank, filled with dirt and water. The men, silent in their determination, stabbed their paddles deep into the churning water and pulled to a more stable shore. Here we made camp and dried things. No one was hurt. Only a few bundles were damaged.

I was glad your father was on shore for no one could blame him for making another mistake.

Papa explained to the captains he had traveled this far up the river, the farthest almost any white man had ever come. They were pleased as their chief Jefferson wished to know how far other white men had traveled on the Missouri. The captains called the stream Charbonneau Creek for him.

Papa wore a huge smile all evening. His only complaint was he had no buffalo meat to make *boudin blanc* for his companions.

"Did you see any more white bears?" Pomp badgered.

"No, not yet, but I wish you could have seen the buffalo calf that followed us one day."

"Did you keep him?"

"No," Sacagawea explained. *"We did not eat him either. It happened this way."*

I was walking with Captain Lewis to a hilltop. The wind was too strong for the canoes to move so we had stopped. The captain walked ahead. Seaman ran here and there, scaring rabbits and snapping at prairie dogs. He played a game with these creatures. He would chase one to its burrow and then try to dig it out. The prairie dog would pop up from another hole and chatter at him. Seaman would then run to that hole and begin digging. Never once did he catch any prairie dogs, but he enjoyed the chase.

This afternoon Seaman came across a baby buffalo. The calf bellowed in fright and ran toward us. I could not see its mother anywhere. The calf trailed behind us as if we were its mother now. Captain Lewis ordered Seaman to leave it alone. Reluctantly, he obeyed but kept his eye on it just in case the captain changed his mind.

From the top of the hill we could see the country spread before us. The captain pointed to the great herds of buffalo and elk. My eyes were pulled west, however, like the captains' magic needle, which always aims to the star of the north. I had hoped to see the Shining Mountains but saw only rolling hills stretching west. In my heart I knew we would not see them yet, but still I hoped. The captains were as eager as I to see these mountains, which they called the Rocky Mountains. They wished to be beyond them when Coldmaker returned for another winter.

"What happened to the baby buffalo?" Pomp asked.

"He ran down the hill, away from our camp. In the distance I saw a wolf slipping through the brush. He scented the calf and was moving toward it. I do not know if the calf escaped to join the herd or provided food for a *litter of hungry wolf pups.*"

For many days after we found the baby buffalo our eyes were red with hurt. The winds pushed against our canoes and blew fine dust into our eyes. The men complained, but there was nothing to be done. The dust whirled and swirled and covered us. We ate dust in our food. We swallowed dust in our water. Captain Clark gave me a white handkerchief to fashion a mask for your face to keep off the dust. It did little good.

We reached the mouth of the River of Yellow Stones where it meets the Missouri. The captains were pleased to be there. They wrote in their books and Captain Clark added the river to his map. Everywhere there were animals. Buffalo, deer, elk, beaver, antelope, and birds beyond imagination. The buffalo and elk had not been hunted for some time and showed no fear of us. We could walk near them as they grazed. They did not yet have their summer meat and fat. The hunters killed three or four and Papa made *boudin blanc*. The smell attracted a wolf pack. They circled the camp, howling with hunger. The men tried to ignore them, but they frequently looked beyond the glow of the campfires at the eyes glinting in the firelight.

Monsieur Cruzatte brought out his fiddle. The men danced until late, so happy were they to have reached the River of Yellow Stones. For them, it was an important part of their journey completed. For me, it meant we were truly getting closer to my home. I hid my excitement as it might displease your father, but I shared my joy with you, Pomp, when we were alone. Inside my spirit danced like a bluestem on a gentle breeze.

We saw more bear tracks. None of the hunters had yet killed one.

Captain Lewis kept Seaman with him for fear a bear might attack him, but one evening the dog wandered from camp. Long into the night Captain Lewis awaited his return, often leaving his sleeping robe to put a stick on the fire. He slept little, I know, for I was awake often, too. My stomach hurt and I tried to lie so as to stop it. This did little good. Yet I dared not tell anyone for fear of halting the expedition. Each day must carry us farther up the river.

Seaman came leaping into camp at dawn. He licked Captain Lewis's hand over and over. The captain rubbed Seaman's mane of black hair and held his face in his hands to scold him. But the look on Seaman's face was such Captain Lewis only laughed. I wondered where Seaman had been, for he had the scent of wolves on him. Had he found a wolf mate?

Captain Lewis carried a round metal watch, which told him the white man's time. You enjoyed listening to its sound like a woodpecker's tapping. The dust had entered it and the sound stopped. He frowned when he held it. I could not understand this watch with the lines that traveled in a circle. Your father tried to explain it to me. For a Shoshoni, one day is like another unless an event happens to mark it in your memory. Like the day a white bear died.

I was not with Captain Lewis when he met his white bear. He told the story at the campfire the evening it happened. Your father put his story into the words of the Hidatsa so I could understand. From the captain's talking hands, as he told the story, I understood much of it.

He was walking along the shore with one man, hunting buffalo. They spotted two bears feeding and shot at them. They each hit a bear. One white bear disappeared into the brush. The other wounded bear was not so cowardly. He stood on his feet and roared at Captain Lewis. Before the captain could reload his rifle, the bear charged. Captain Lewis ran with the bear growling fiercely behind him. His gunshot slowed the bear so he had time to reload. The other man reloaded as well. They shot again. The bear fell.

Captain Lewis said it was much bigger than any bears they had in his country and it weighed more than York. York laughed at this and imitated a growling bear so well Seaman barked at him.

The captain bragged that, even though the Indians feared the white bear, it was no match for his rifle. I said nothing, knowing they had killed a bear of only a few years. I hoped no one would be hurt when they faced a grizzly of many years. Captain Lewis might tell a different story then.

"Is that the bear whose claw I wear?" Pomp asked.

Sacagawea fingered the curved claw dangling from his neck like a crescent moon.

"No," she replied. "We met that bear later."

"Tell me about it, please," Pomp begged.

"When the time comes." Sacagawea sighed. "When the time comes. A story is like a tipi. You have to put up the right poles at the right time or it will not stand."

"Like York did the first time?"

"Yes, but only the first time."

chapter 12

The next morning the sky was gray and a storm burst upon them. Sacagawea, Pomp, and Charbonneau huddled in the small cabin at the stern of the flatboat as Sacagawea continued her story.

One afternoon Captain Lewis returned to camp with the curved horn of a mountain sheep. Inside I smiled, for leaping sheep live only in high places where their enemies cannot tread. The People hunted these sheep by surrounding a flock and forcing some to fall. The captains were excited by the horn. Captain Lewis described the sheep he had seen high on a cliff. He had shot at them, but they were too far away for his shot to harm them. The captains had never before seen such horn and sheep, and wrote about it in their books. They saved the horn to send to Mr. Jefferson.

Animals remained plentiful and the men shot only what we needed. This afternoon an antelope herd fleeing from a wolf pack leaped into the river and attempted to swim across and escape their pursuers.

Seaman rode with us in the white pirogue. He

barked and rocked the boat he was so excited. Finally, the hunt was too much and he jumped into the river, too.

He swam toward an antelope, its eyes wide with fear. Suddenly Seaman swerved, for he was hit by the antelope's feet kicking beneath the water. Seaman had never before hunted antelope this way and did not know the wolves' tricks. He stopped and watched a wolf drag an antelope underwater by its throat. In perfect imitation he grabbed another antelope and pulled it underwater. The antelope stopped struggling. Seaman proudly swam to shore with his catch.

Captain Lewis rewarded him with tugs on his ears and much praise. We ate roasted antelope haunch for our evening meal.

Sacagawea stopped and smiled.

"Seaman was a very intelligent dog. When he made a mistake, he never did it again."

"What mistake did he make?" Pomp asked.

"He tried to kill a beaver the same way he attacked the antelope."

"What happened?"

"The beaver is as at home in the water as an antelope is at home on land. Seaman saw one swimming and jumped into the water to catch it. Suddenly the beaver spun around, snapped its sharp yellow teeth, and almost bit Seaman on the nose. Never again did Seaman try to catch a live beaver."

Each day we saw bighorn sheep, but none could be killed for the captains to inspect. I told them they would find many, many more when we reached the Shining Mountains. I also showed a bush upon which still hung a few yellow berries from last summer. I picked them and gave them to Captain Clark who smiled as he enjoyed them, sharing the handful with your father and me.

Finding this plant pleased me much as it grew in great numbers in the mountains and was one more sign we were nearing my home.

Even so, Coldmaker was not through with us. One morning we awoke to snow covering the plains. Flowers poked their colorful heads through the white blanket. The cottonwoods had leaves as large as geese eggs powdered with snow. The wind was violent and chilled us. Even so the land was of great beauty. I remember many mornings as a child when snow fell like this. To me it was another sign I was closer to The People. One good thing about the cold is it killed some mosquitoes. Later, however, others returned to revenge their lost companions.

A man was ill with the ache of the bones. Captain Lewis tended to him as he did all of the sick or injured men. He had a box of medicines from which he took powders and liquids to heal the men. Every day someone hurt himself or became sick. Backs were injured pulling the canoes against the current. Toes were stubbed on rocks and roots. Many men complained of stomachaches, especially after drinking unclear water. I watched Captain Lewis tend to those needing help. I wished to tell him our remedies, but he did not want to learn our ways in medicines.

My own stomachache had dulled. Occasionally I felt a pain stabbing my insides. I did not complain, so determined was I not to cause any delay. I chewed the bark of the willow tree as did the Shoshoni when they had a pain. This eased my ache.

Each day we proceeded, either on land or on the water. We had been gone one moon from the village of the Mandan when Captain Clark killed his first grizzly bear, the one whose claw you wear.

"Did you see him him shoot the bear?" Pomp asked.

No, but we heard shots from the shore. The men thought we were being attacked by Indians and they grabbed their weapons. Then we heard Captain Clark shout from shore and he pulled the canoes in to him. At his feet lay a huge white bear, twice the size of the first one killed.

York lay down in the sand beside the bear and stretched his hands up over his head. Even so he barely measured from the fingertips to his toes the same as the bear. Drouillard skinned the bear and gave the fur to Captain Clark. He pushed his fingers through ten bullet holes. Five bullets had hit the bear's lungs. Still he had the strength to swim to a sandbar.

The captains ordered the bear oil placed into a cask and saved. Papa was pleased, for bear oil is best for frying *boudin blanc*. The meat we shared between the men.

Captain Clark removed the bear's claws. Nine he kept for himself. This one he gave to you, Pomp, signing the word brave.

"What did he mean?" Pomp asked.

"That all through your life you must be as brave as the great grizzly: fearsome in battle and just as hard to kill."

chapter
13

Wisps of fog floated over the Missouri. The flatboat was tied to a tree on an island where they were to spend the night. Sacagawea and Pomp walked along the shore. Sacagawea dug beneath a pile of driftwood and pulled up five roots.

"Are these what you found for the captains?" Pomp asked with his usual curiosity.

"Yes, these and many more kinds. Captain Lewis enjoyed them, but he truly disliked the white apples I cooked."

"Pommes blancs *like you cook for us?*" Pomp asked.

"Oui," *Sacagawea answered.*

"But I love those!" Pomp exclaimed. "Especially roasted."

"I served them many ways for the men. York and Captain Clark took pleasure in them and often asked me to gather more. In the Shoshoni way I boiled them in soup or mashed them with buffalo meat or peeled and ate them raw as the white bears do. Never once did Captain Lewis like them."

"The white bears ate white apples?" Pomp queried.

"Many times we found white apples in a bear's gullet."

Sacagawea rested on a cottonwood log. Pomp sat beside her. The sun slid from the sky as dusk approached. Smells from the cooking fire drifted to them as she spoke.

Not every day did something exciting happen. Always there was the wind and the weather. The captains were pleased with their hunting and we ate buffalo, elk, or beaver every meal. As I walked the shore I often saw the great paw prints of the white bear. The captains were eager to challenge the grizzly, convinced the bears were no match for their rifles.

Fog drifted over the river as it does now. I walked with Captain Clark as he hunted. From the hills beyond the river, we saw great herds of buffalo, elk, deer, and antelope. As always, packs of wolves skulked around the edges of the herds, waiting for the young, old, or injured to fall behind and provide them with a meal.

Captain Clark was eager to shoot elk because Captain Lewis needed the skins to make his boat. In my mind I pictured a round bullboat. This we would use past the great falls of Missouri where the river tumbles over a steep cliff. I yearned to reach the falls, for then we were not many days' journey from the mountains and home.

We made camp to dry wet things. Captain Lewis

paced at his fire, for the last two canoes had not caught up with us. He was concerned for them. Finally, they appeared and immediately told their terrifying story.

They had seen a huge bear resting in an open place not far from the river. The six best hunters among them hid behind a small hill and approached the bear unseen until they were as near as we are to the fire.

Two held back their shots, for by now the men knew the danger of attacking a white bear. Four fired at the same time. The bear roared his terrible roar and stood up. Bellowing, he charged the men. The two remaining hunters fired. Their shots struck the bear, only angering him more. He chased the men, who scattered like the down of milkweed. Two fled to the canoes and pulled away from shore, calling to their companions to swim to them. The other four, cut off from the river by the bear, hid in the willows and reloaded their guns.

Again, they fired at the bear, the bullets striking him. The smoke from their guns revealed where they hid. The bear routed them, almost caught two who dropped their guns and jumped off a cliff into the river.

The bear, even more angered that his tormentors were escaping, leaped from the cliff into the water after them. Roaring and splashing he reached out his long arms, stretched out his sharp claws, and just as the bear's claws reached a man's back, one of the men on shore put a bullet into the bear's skull. The bear tumbled dead into the river. The men pulled him out and found every shot had hit the bear, and all from eight directions.

After this, the captains ordered the men to be more careful and not shoot the white bears unless the bears endangered them. At last, the captains learned to respect the grizzlies as the Indians do. Captain Lewis remarked that from now on he would rather face two angry Indian warriors than one white bear.

*E*ach day we traveled brought us closer to the
great falls and the Shining Mountains. Through
hand talk and Papa's translations, the captains questioned me about the country through which we
passed. I could not tell them anything as my Hidatsa
captors had not come this way. Yet I could explain to
them the nature of the land and how its changes meant
we were approaching the mountains.

Every chance that came, the captains climbed the
highest hill and looked west. Sometimes we went with
them. Sometimes we stayed in camp. I did my chores
and cared for you. Yet each time I was anxious to see
their expressions for I could tell if they had seen the
mountains or not.

This was when snakes crawled from their winter
burrows in the rocks and sunned themselves. I tried to
warn the captains of rattlesnakes, but I did not have
the sign or the word for it. I made a *SSSSSTTTTT*
sound and shook my fingers.

Captain Clark understood. He pointed to you,

Pomp, and signed your birth. I remembered the crushed rattlesnake rattles he had me drink to help bring you into the world.

Even with the warning, Captain Clark narrowly missed being bitten by a snake. We were walking with him as the men pulled the canoes with long ropes of elk skin. The wind was strong but contrary and would not let the men raise the sails. Up to their knees and hips, they struggled against the river, men pulling in the front while one guided the boats with a rope attached to the rear. Your papa hated this towing and tried to find any excuse to get out of it. The other men resented this, and he soon did not argue. Perhaps he remembered that he did not wish to anger the captains, especially after almost losing the white pirogue.

Captain Clark saw a lone bull elk browsing. He crept through the sagebrush to shoot it. Captain Lewis wished its hide for his special boat. I stayed behind, hushing you so the elk was not alerted.

I saw a coiled rattlesnake sleeping on a wide rock. Captain Clark, his eyes on the elk, did not see the snake and was stepping toward it. I froze, not knowing if I should shout and frighten off the elk or if the captain would hear the rattles and avoid the snake.

Just as he was about to step on the snake, a cry burst from my mouth.

"Aiiiee! Captain!" I yelled.

The snake raised its head to strike. Its tail waved,

the rattles clicking loudly. Captain Clark jumped back just as the rattlesnake struck, missing his leg by the width of your hand.

My heart beat quickly, for a rattlesnake's bite is often deadly. I knew the Shoshoni way of cutting open the wound and sucking out the poison, but sometimes that does not save the person.

York killed a snake near the camp that evening. Captain Lewis examined the snake, counting even its belly scales. He wrote words in his book about the snake. On his map Captain Clark named a creek Rattlesnake Creek for the many snakes crawling there.

We had survived bear attacks, snake attacks, thirsty mosquitoes, and now fire became our enemy.

"One that other Indians set?" Pomp asked.

"No, our own," Sacagawea answered.

Every night the men prepared three fires around which they cooked, talked, ate, and rested. In each group one man cooked. Others gathered wood for their fire. York and I did these chores for our fire.

This night was no different, although the men kept the fires small for a strong wind blew, sending sparks racing through the camp.

York and I set up the tipi near a cottonwood tree. The wind's fingers tried to push the lodge over. I showed York how to stake the lodge properly with a ring of stones around the bottom and defeat the wind.

Late in the night a man standing guard yelled for

us to leave the lodge. I grabbed you and dashed through the opening. The cottonwood above the tipi had caught fire and blazed brightly.

I handed you to Captain Clark. York and I with Drouillard and Papa unstaked the tipi and pulled it away just as a burning branch fell into the circle where the tipi stood. Without the warning, the branch would have crushed us. We would be in the spirit world.

The wind did not stop. We moved the lodge far from the cottonwood into the open. Fire leaped from the burning branch onto dry logs and spread. Sparks and glowing coals swirled into the sky. The world became as day. All night we battled the flying fires. Holes as big as your fist burned into our tipi, holes which took me much time to repair.

We left early in the morning straight into the teeth of the wind. It blew from the west, and surely had passed over The People. Finally, it faded. A gentle rain trailed behind it. You laughed as I held your face into the sprinkle as this was your first rain.

Captain Clark killed four deer. We needed the meat to eat and the skins to repair the tipi and for clothes and moccasins. As we rode in the pirogue, I chewed a doeskin to soften it to make clothes for you. At each evening's fire I stitched until my fingers ached.

The man named Colter watched me make moccasins. He signed I should teach him. Never before had any man except York wished to do a woman's work. If he learned, I thought, he could join York and me making moccasins. With thirty feet to cover we had many to make.

Colter's first attempt was clumsy. I had seen him shoot a rifle. His fingers were strong and steady. But his stitches were uneven and his moccasins would have leaked like a grass basket with holes in it. Yet he was determined. By the next winter, the men begged him to make his fine moccasins for them.

The next day as I sewed, my stitches were for Seaman.

"You made moccasins for him?" Pomp joked.

"Yes," Sacagawea answered. *"He needed them when we neared the great falls where the prickly pear cactus rule the country. That day, my needle and sinew kept Seaman alive."*

"How, Mama?"

We had seen many beavers. They fed on the bark of the willows and carried branches back to their burrows in the riverbanks. The men shot four beaver, one which floated in the water. Captain Lewis sent Seaman to fetch it, thinking the beaver dead from its wounds. Seaman obeyed and leaped into the river.

But the beaver was still alive! Seaman lunged toward it. The beaver swirled and attacked him. Wary of the beaver's sharp teeth, Seaman turned. The beaver bit him in the hind leg. Yelping, Seaman swam to shore, trailing blood.

Captain Lewis dashed into the water. Cradling Seaman like a baby, he carried him out. He lay Seaman on an elk hide and ordered his medicine chest. Blood flowed from the wound in spurts. The beaver's teeth had sliced an artery carrying the heart's blood. The captain sprinkled powder on the wound. Still the blood flowed. Desperate, he tore a strip from his shirt and pressed it to the wound. The bandage turned red from Seaman's blood.

I knelt by the dog and held his head. He looked at me with his huge eyes, whimpering as his life seeped into the sand.

I remembered my mother, Bright Eyes, using her bone needle and sinew thread to stitch closed a wound my sister Tall Grass got when her black stone knife slipped and she cut her leg.

I called to Papa to bring my needle and thread to me quickly. With hand motions I told Captain Lewis what I planned to do. He shook his head and pressed harder on the wound.

Seaman yelped and jerked his leg away. He bared his teeth at the captain, something he had never done before.

Once more I showed Captain Lewis what I wished to do. He agreed. We changed places. He held Seaman's head and stroked it.

Talking to Seaman as I do you when you are hurt, I soothed him until he relaxed. I gently removed the bloodstained cloth and pinched the wound shut. As if I were making moccasins for Chief Jefferson himself, I carefully stitched the wound closed. Seaman made not a sound.

Seaman slept in our lodge next to Captain Lewis. He fed him water from a spoon and talked to him softly through the night. In the morning, Seaman raised his head and licked the captain's hand. Like the sun shining after a thunderstorm, a smile spread across Captain Lewis's face.

Seaman would live.

"In appreciation for this kindness to his dog, Captain Lewis named a swift flowing river in my honor, Sacagawea River. Maybe when you are a grown man, you will hunt along this river and remember your mother."

"I will never forget you, Mama. Never," Pomp stated emphatically.

"Not even when Captain Clark teaches you the wonders of the white man's world?"

"Never!" he exclaimed.

Sacagawea smiled to herself. Never is a long time, she thought.

chapter 15

"**M**ama, tell me more about Seaman," Pomp begged the next day.

His hair was as black as yours. Each evening I picked the burrs and traveling seeds from his fur. His wound healed. Within five suns, he walked again, although with a limp. Captain Lewis made him return to his sleeping place in front of the tipi flap. Just as the captains posted guards each night around the camp, so Seaman guarded our lodge.

This was a good thing, for he saved our lives. It was something that had never happened to The People or we would have had a story about it.

"Why do the Shoshoni have so many stories?" Pomp asked.

Sacagawea hesitated before answering.

"The People do not write things down in books as the white men do. We keep our stories in our heads. Some stories are funny. Some are sad. Many teach lessons to our young people. Others tell of important events in the tribe."

"Like when you were captured?"

"My capture was not important enough for a story," she said.

"It is to me," Pomp announced. *"That is why you are telling it now. But I do not know if your story is funny, sad, or teaches a lesson. Maybe it is all stories in one."* He grinned and nodded his head.

You are probably right, my petit *French Shoshoni,* Sacagawea thought, and she continued her story.

Each night the men fell asleep quickly, exhausted from their labors. They spent much time in cold water, pulling the canoes with elk-skin ropes. The ropes, old and worn, often broke, plunging the men face first into the frigid water.

The river ran clearer. Many more were the rocks. The mud, which had tugged off our moccasins, was much less. Sitting in the pirogue, I saw the difference in the Missouri. Instead of being wide and flat like a lake, it flowed like a stream. Each day we struggled over more shallow rapids.

As tired as the men were, they were happy also, for the captains had climbed up the steep banks to a hilltop. From there they saw the Shining Mountains for the first time. This brought great joy, for it meant they had almost reached their goal of finding the beginnings of the Missouri. In their tongue, they called them the Rocky Mountains. They spoke of snow shining on the mountaintops. I had Papa explain to them this is why The People call them the Shining Mountains, for on their highest peaks the snows never melt.

Both men gazed toward the setting sun for a long time this evening.

I felt great joy, too. My journey was almost at an end. My people were only a few days' journey ahead.

A few nights after seeing the mountains, we camped on flat ground near the river. The broken cliffs reaching to the river's edge made finding a place to sleep difficult.

I did not fall asleep immediately. Captain Clark had brought me a moccasin he found at an abandoned Indian camp. I signed to him the moccasin was not made by the Shoshoni but by the Minnetree who sometimes lived near us in the foothills of the mountains. He was pleased to learn this.

This night as always Seaman slept by the tipi flap. I walked around the edge of the camp before sleeping. The air was crisp. Frost formed on the grass. Stars sparkled like tiny suns reflecting off a clear stream. I looked at the star that never moves, the one the captains call the star of the north. At last, I wrapped myself in my buffalo robe and slept.

We were awakened by a shout. Louder though was the bellow of an enraged buffalo.

The night was dark. All but one fire had burned low. Captain Clark opened the tipi flap. Seaman exploded from his resting place. He barked fiercely at the charging buffalo.

I hugged you close, fearing what the frantic buffalo would do when it crashed into our lodge. Seaman lunged at the buffalo, now not more than a man's length away. The buffalo, startled by this black wolflike creature attacking him, snorted and turned, his tail knocking the flap from the captain's hand. The buffalo bellowed as it ran, scrambling up a rocky hillside with Seaman chasing it.

Everyone was awake. Some held blazing torches. It took the captains much time to finally understand what had happened. Papa explained it to me.

The buffalo, a great bull, had swum across the river toward our camp. He trampled the white pirogue before dashing into the camp. In the torchlight we saw where his sharp hooves had missed the heads of the sleeping men by less than the length of your arm.

No one was injured. In the morning we found the bull had crushed York's rifle. Captain Lewis said something about the white pirogue's being menaced by an evil spirit he called a "genie."

I do not know what a "genie" is but the white pirogue did have more troubles than the other canoes.

"Did this genie come again?" Pomp asked.

"Yes, the very next day. We almost lost the white pirogue."

"How?" queried Pomp.

The river now was much different. The Missouri here looks like the coffee Papa drinks. The banks are far apart and cloaked with trees. Where we were, the river was clear and shallow. Tall cliffs with towers of rocks rose above us on both sides. The men, not even wearing moccasins, for the thick mud sucked them off their feet, waded in the water and pulled the canoes. Sometimes a man slipped and disappeared beneath the river, then surfaced, sputtering. They toiled up to their armpits in the freezing water. To add to our misery heavy rains fell. This did not stop the swarming mosquitoes and gnats, which surrounded us in black clouds.

We made little distance struggling against the current and the cold. Yet not once did the men complain. Where the captains would lead, they would follow.

We were riding in the white pirogue to which the captains had attached their best rope. This rope was not of elk skin but of strong plant fibers. The men struggled against the current, slipping and sliding but gaining on the river. You and I were riding, as the banks were too steep for me to walk. All at once the rope snapped. One end whipped back like a striking snake. The current grabbed the bow of the pirogue and smashed it into a rock. The waves bucked the small boat like a boy on an untamed horse. Water splashed in, and for one long moment I thought we would flip over.

But the current held us against the rock until two men scrambled out and pulled us to shore.

The captains, seeing how tired the men were, called an early halt. Great fires were built of driftwood and the men soon warmed.

We camped on an island and Captain Clark took me with him to look at an Indian camp he had discovered. The lodges were made of bent sticks and covered with bark. We found nothing I could recognize from my tribe.

The island bloomed with roses. Chokecherries were in blossom as were the bright yellow flowers of the prickly pear cactus. Never before had we seen so many of these plants. This day they looked beautiful, but soon we learned to hate them.

"But why, Mama?" Pomp wanted to know.

"That is the next lodgepole of the story, Pomp. Before this time, the wind and the current had been our enemies. Now the prickly pears attacked us with the ferocity of white bears."

chapter 16

Around the campfire Charbonneau, Sacagawea, and Pomp ate the meal she had prepared. The sky blazed with the setting sun. Golden light tinted the clouds from orange to pink. Overhead, early stars glimmered.

"Papa, won't you tell me some of the story?" Pomp asked.

"No, no, there is not much for me to tell. Mama has been sharing the story. Let her continue."

Sacagawea said, "Papa, let my tongue rest. You tell Pomp about your encounter with the white bear."

"You hunted the grizzly, Papa?"

"Yes, but he hunted me as well." Charbonneau chuckled. He tapped the side of his head with his finger. "Those bears are smart. But not smarter than your papa . . ."

As with almost every day, the wind blew hard against us. We were tired. Our backs and arms burned with an aching fire. Our feet were cut from the sharp stones in the river. Still we pulled on.

This day, however, I was sent out with the hunting party.

Captain Lewis wished to hunt, as we saw much more game now than we had seen recently. He was especially interested in elk, for he needed many skins to cover his metal boat.

"Metal boat?" Pomp interrupted. "What metal boat?"

Charbonneau burst into laughter. "In the red pirogue Captain Lewis had the skeleton for a boat he wished to build. You know the bullboats of the Mandan with their willow frames covered with buffalo hides?"

Pomp nodded his head.

Captain Lewis had a special metal frame made for the boat he wished to build to carry us along the river once we were past the great falls. To cover it he needed at least twenty elk skins. Seeing so many elk made him determined to hunt for skins. We also needed meat, for when we pulled the boats as we did, we grew very, very hungry.

I was hunting with Drouillard along the shore. Here many willows and cottonwoods grew. Sometimes the land was open, sometimes closed in by brush. We shot a deer and marked its place so we could find it later.

Drouillard was off to my left when I heard a great crashing sound. Then I heard the roar with which we were too familiar. I saw Drouillard burst from the bushes. Behind him galloped a white bear. They were both running toward me.

I cocked my rifle and hid behind a tree so the bear would not see me. The ground shook as the bear approached. Drouillard ducked behind another tree and began to reload his rifle.

Just as the bear was past my tree, I fired my rifle into the air to distract him. The bear whirled around at the sound and chased me! I ran, dodging here and there like a jackrabbit. *Mon Dieu,* I prayed that Drouillard would quickly reload his gun.

I ran into some thick brush, dropped to my belly, and crawled as far as I could. The bear roared with anger, ripping away bushes to get me. I crawled and crawled until I was almost out the other side.

Then I heard a single shot. My heart almost stopped. No one had ever killed a white bear with one shot. I knew Drouillard was as good a shot as Captain Lewis, but to kill a white bear with only one bullet. . . . Impossible!

But I could no longer hear the bear growling. Maybe he had turned and was after Drouillard, I thought.

I crawled out of the bushes. I reloaded my rifle, my shaking hands spilling only a little powder. When I was ready, I ran around the clump of bushes, rifle aimed ahead.

Charbonneau stopped to relight his pipe, which had gone out.

Pomp impatiently tugged on his buckskin sleeve. "Was the bear dead?" he asked.

Charbonneau grinned.

With his one shot, my friend Drouillard had killed the great white bear. He had hit it in the head, the only place one bullet can stop such a monster. I clapped him on the shoulder, thanking him for his most excellent aim.

"He saved your life," Sacagawea said.

Charbonneau gazed at her for a long moment.

"Yes, he did," Charbonneau admitted. "Yet around the fire that evening Drouillard claimed it was my shot that startled the bear so he could reload and have a perfect shot. I did give him the best of my boudin blanc for the rest of the journey."

Sacagawea said, "That was the day before the first long rest. How we needed it."

Charbonneau tapped the remains of his tobacco out of his pipe and stood up. "I will talk with the men now while you continue the tale," he said.

"Will you tell it tonight, Mama?" Pomp asked.

"I will, for it was like the lull before a storm. Remember at home how we could feel a storm coming across the prairie long before it reached us?"

"Oui. The air became still and the birds stopped singing. The wind began slow and then faster and faster until the thunder and lightning crashed around us and rain poured down on us," Pomp said.

"You sound like a storyteller yourself." She smiled. "And this is good, for like me, you do not know how to make the leaves in books speak to you. Captain Clark will

teach you. But never forget the Shoshoni way of telling sto-
ries. This way we will never die as long as our stories are
told."

"*Well, Mama, what happened next?*" Pomp wanted
to know.

Everyone needed to rest and the captains realized
this. However, we could not find a satisfactory place
for a long encampment until soon after the bear chased
Papa.

It was in the first days of *Bu'Hisea-Mea'a,* The
Budding Moon. We had reached a fork in the river.
The south branch flowed from the direction of the star
of the north. Its waters ran strong and fast like those of
the river we had been traveling. The bottom was
muddy and the water colored the same. The men
believed this to be the Missouri and wished to continue journeying on it.

The other stream flowed much faster and was
much clearer. The river bottom was stony. I was
reminded of the fast-flowing streams of my home.
Both captains felt that this river was the real Missouri,
"The River That Scolds All Others" as the Hidatsa
called it.

I agreed with them and I signed I believed this river
led to the mountains. They questioned me as to whether
I recognized any marks on the land. I climbed a high hill
with the captains and looked west. There stood row
upon row of snow-covered mountains. Somewhere in

those shining mountains my family lived. I pointed to the mountains, smiled, and nodded my head, for I knew this was the white man's sign for yes.

We camped on a point of land where the two rivers became one.

The men talked and pointed to the north fork. The captains talked and pointed to the south fork. After much talk it was decided the men who were too weary to travel would stay, make camp, and rest.

I was eager to continue but knew it was better for me to rest, too. We had been two moons on our journey and we would certainly reach The People before the first snow fell again. But only if the captains made the right decision. I felt sorrow for them, for I knew that even as cheerful as the men were, the journey was telling on their strength. There was still laughter around the fires at night, but not as much as before. Cruzatte played his fiddle, but not as often. If the captains picked the wrong river and traveled many days up it only to find out they had made a mistake, the remaining heart of the men might give out and the captains might be forced to end their journey.

I shivered at night worrying about this, and decided if such a disaster happened, we would run away and make our way to The People on our own. I began saving pieces of meat and drying it for jerky. I stored a pouch of bear fat in my parfleche. Berries were coming into season and we could survive on them until we reached the mountains.

Would Papa chase after us, I wondered? Once we reached the mountains would we be able to find The People? I pushed these bad thoughts from my mind and sought to be ready if we must flee.

The captains sent men in canoes and on foot up each branch the following day. Those who stayed in camp prepared the elk skins for Captain Lewis's metal boat. Others made new clothing from deer skins. They were not soft, but all the men needed them. Their first clothes had worn to rags. I repaired the tipi, made moccasins, cared for you, and pondered how to convince the captains which way to turn.

The men returned with news of what they had seen. Neither group had found any true indication of which river was the one to follow. So around the fires that night many words were shared.

The captains decided the next day they would each lead a group up a river. They would travel for a day and a half and return to this camp to share what they had found. Captain Lewis would take six men and venture up the north fork. Captain Clark and York would travel with four men up the south fork. When they returned they would decide which river they would continue on.

"Didn't Papa want to go?" Pomp asked.

He did, but the captains and the men wished him to stay to cook for them. Captain Lewis spent much time making a pack for his back. I laughed inside, for clearly he had never attempted this before. He could not carry with him all he wished to take. I shared with him my pouch of bear fat. He smiled his thanks and placed it in his pack after he had removed other things. Upon his return he instructed Papa to tell me he had roasted plump prairie dogs in the fat and the flavor pleased him much.

Captain Clark returned in two days, but we waited and worried for two more until Captain Lewis came back. While we waited the men dried things and packed them into the canoes so we would be ready to leave as soon as Captain Lewis returned.

Late in the afternoon we heard Seaman's bark. He bounded into camp with Captain Lewis and his weary men trailing behind him. The captains talked among themselves for a long time, then talked with the men. Although I understood few of the words, I knew the captains now believed what I had told them. The south fork was the way to the mountains.

Yet all the men, Papa included, were convinced otherwise. They wished to travel up the north fork. Monsieur Cruzatte, who knew the Missouri as well he knew the strings on his fiddle, strongly believed the north fork to be the real river.

Such was the power of the captains and the trust the men placed in them, because we prepared to turn the canoes up the south fork.

My heart smiled.

17

I wished to begin in the morning, but the captains decided they had too many things to carry. They had planned to send men downstream with more things for Mr. Jefferson, but changed their minds. Instead, they would leave much behind, things that would be a burden to carry over the mountains.

Monsieur Cruzatte showed them how fur trappers hid things from their enemies in an underground cache.

First, a small circle of grass is cut from the earth. A shallow hole as deep as your arm is dug. Then the hole is widened and made much deeper, taller than a man. This hole is lined with elk skins.

Into this the captains placed many things. The skins of our bears and beaver, axes, kegs of Mandan maize, tin cups, beaver traps, spare rifles, and heavy tools. The skins were folded over the cache. The small circle was placed back again. All signs of the cache were brushed away and the earth dumped into the stream. Unless you had seen the men digging, you would not have guessed what things lay in the earth.

The red pirogue was taken to an island in the river and tied with the best elk-skin ropes. Captain Lewis burned his marks into some trees with a hot iron so he would recognize this place once again.

As I watched these preparations, I understood the captains cached things to avoid carrying them and they planned to return home to their country this way.

The men prepared from dawn to sunset. I thought we would leave when the sun rose again. However, Captain Lewis became very sick that evening. To ease his pain I broke many small chokecherry twigs into boiling water. This black water I signed would be good for his intestines. Instead, he chose to take his medicines. His powders worked a little, but not enough for him to join the celebration at the fires that evening when Monsieur Cruzatte played his fiddle and the men danced until the moon stood overhead.

In the morning, even though he was still suffering, Captain Lewis and four men walked overland to the great falls the Hidatsa had described. When he found the falls, Captain Lewis would send a man back to Captain Clark, who followed along the river. The Hidatsa said it was only a half day's portage around the falls.

For us, Pomp, we traveled the river with Captain Clark, still in the heavy white pirogue.

Later I learned what happened to Captain Lewis as

he made his way to the falls. I had no knowledge of the next days, for this is when I came close to joining my ancestors.

"You almost died, Mama?" Pomp asked. "You never told me this before."

"There are many things I am telling you now for the first time. You are growing older and will soon stop being a young boy. You are going to join the tribe of Captain Clark, not as a child, but as what The People call 'a becoming man.' This is why I tell you the story of our journey so you will know what wonders you saw as a baby and how brave you became."

"But how did you almost die?"

A sickness made my fingers and arms quiver. My body had fever, more fever than I had ever known. My breath came hard and my heart beat as if it were a drum. In my dreams, my mother, Bright Morning, held me and bathed my brow with cool water.

Captain Clark became much concerned. He took a sharp knife and let out some of my blood. This is the white man's way of purging an evil spirit. He wished me to drink Captain Lewis's medicines, but I refused. I wished to drink what the Shoshoni drank to chase the sickness from their bodies. Papa finally forced me to take the white powder medicines. They made me sleep and eased my pain, but still I burned like a prairie fire.

I lay in the bottom of the pirogue on a pile of buffalo

robes, with you on my breast. Day passed into night, which passed again into day.

One morning I awoke to find Captain Lewis leaning over me. His face was much worried, as was Captain Clark's. My heart worried, too, for if I died, who would feed you and clean you and make you into a Shoshoni warrior?

I did not want to die and struggled against it with all my might. Yet the sickness would not leave my body.

I had a great thirst as if I had not had water for many suns. Captain Lewis sent a man to fetch a bucket of stinking water from a spring. The water smelled of rotten eggs and tasted like blood. I forced myself to drink it, trusting in the healing I had seen Captain Lewis perform on his own men. He also gave me a medicine of bark and white powder.

All day I slept and, when the evening star rose, I awoke. My arms, which before could not hold you, Pomp, for all of their shaking, now grasped you like a drowning man grabs a floating log. My heart beat smoothly once more.

My hunger returned and I felt I could eat a whole buffalo calf. Captain Lewis, however, let me eat only a few small bites of meat.

I slept through the night, my only discomfort being the hunger, which gnawed at my belly.

In the morning I felt like a newborn antelope,

ready to leap and run. The captains were busy building a boat for the land. They called it a wagon and made cottonwood circles on which it was to roll. The canoes would be carried on this wagon and the rest of the equipment would be carried in packs on the men's backs.

They also made another cache, for it was now known the half-day portage would take many suns to complete. The white pirogue with its evil spirit was to be left behind.

I strapped you on my back and went hunting for food to fill my emptiness. I found many white apples, which I ate without cooking. As my belly filled, I felt the world begin to spin. The fever flared and the shaking returned.

Captain Lewis was much angered at your papa, blaming him for my becoming sick again. But it was not Papa's fault. It was mine. Yet I feared he did not wish to blame me for fear of making my condition worse. Captain Lewis gave me his medicines. In the morning I was greatly refreshed and still much with hunger. I ate a little buffalo meat and soup. Now I had the strength to care for you and to make the long walk around the great falls.

Pomp climbed in Sacagawea's lap and huddled close to her. She hugged him tight for a long moment as he whispered, "I am glad you did not go to join your ancestors, Mama."

Tears welled in her eyes. "I am, too, for I would not see you old enough for this journey, nor would I have seen my people again nor the ocean nor the great fish of the ocean. But these things lie ahead in the story. Now, my 'becoming a man,' you must go to sleep. Tomorrow I will tell of prickly pears with claws sharper than the white bear's. And how you were almost lost."

Pomp touched the tip of the claw hanging around his neck. A look of wonder filled his eyes.

"Tomorrow," he said. "Bonne nuit." And he fell asleep in her arms.

18

*I*n the morning Sacagawea continued her story. Captain Clark scouted the route for the portage around the great falls. He placed stakes into the ground to mark the best trail. He decided he would work with the men to carry the equipment around the falls. Captain Lewis went ahead with six men to hunt elk as he needed sixty skins to make his metal boat. He would make a camp at a place he called White Bear Island, named for the tribe of white bears living there.

Captain Clark said the distance was as much as a man could walk from sunup to midday. Yet a man could not truly walk this land that fast. Everywhere the ground was covered with prickly pear cactuses. As soon as one took a step, his foot came down onto cactus needles. The needles shredded the men's moccasins. York, Colter, and I stitched double soles onto the moccasins, but the needles cut through them like a steel knife through liver. The needles tore their deerskin leggings until they looked like a white bear had clawed them.

Mosquitoes attacked the men with a fierceness we had not yet encountered. Poor Seaman howled with the suffering, and his nose was swollen from their bites and his nostrils sometimes plugged.

One day a thunderstorm caught the men between camps. Hailstones as big as your fists beat them, so they hid under the wagon to escape injury. Still, many had great round bruises on their arms and legs.

I remained behind at the first camp until I was strong enough to walk to White Bear Island. The man called Ordway, Papa, York, and I camped there while the men made the portage. York and Ordway hunted, Papa rendered the buffalo fat for Captain Lewis's boat, and I fished and gathered berries.

Each morning the men went with their burdens. They returned bloody from scratches and exhausted from battling the wind and the weather.

Still, they were pleased when they entered camp for they could tell by the smells what we had prepared their meal. York killed us many buffalo. We boiled the hump, stewed the meat, and Papa made *boudin blanc*. I caught trout and served them the Shoshoni way with fresh berries.

After eating, the men collapsed on the ground in their robes, pulled cactus needles from their feet, and slept the sleep of the dead. Captain Clark told us that sometimes the men were so tired they fell asleep pulling the wagon.

Finally the last load was ready, and we left camp. I was excited, for now I would see the five great falls, which the captains told about. We walked all day, the sun beating down, the mosquitoes and prickly pears attacking. These things I ignored. My eyes were set on the Shining Mountains.

Late in the afternoon we were with Papa, York, and Captain Clark. The men were too tired to make the journey in one day, so we left them to rest and eat while we went ahead to the camp on White Bear Island.

We stopped by the first fall, its water crashing and splashing over the rocks. The falls fell from the height of the tallest cottonwood tree. Never before had I heard water roar with such force or send up so much spray. Rainbows arched in the air. I looked forward to sharing this wonder with The People when we joined them.

My eyes saw the thundercloud first and I pointed it out to Captain Clark. At the same time the wind came up so strong it almost blew us over the edge and into the tumbling river.

Captain Clark led us to a narrow ravine to escape the storm's fury. We ducked under a flat rock sticking out of the wall, like the roof of the winter fort. I took you out of your cradleboard and took off your clothes to keep them dry. I held you tight, for the crashing thunder made your eyes large with worry.

In the ravine we listened to the wind howl above us. When the first showers fell, we stayed dry under our rock. Then the rain fell more violently than any I had ever seen. Hail pounded on our rock.

Suddenly we heard the roaring of water racing down the ravine. We scrambled to reach higher ground before we drowned. Within moments water sucked at my moccasins. Papa went first and grabbed my hand, but he then stood as if frozen by the Coldmaker himself. Shouting, Captain Clark pushed me ahead of him up the slippery slope. Papa finally pulled us to the top. The water was at Captain Clark's waist before we could get up the hill. I feared he would be sucked down, but he struggled up behind us. In the time it takes to tell you this, Pomp, the water had risen higher than a man can reach above his head.

We could not remain cold and wet on the open ground, so we ran back to the camp as fast as we could. Captain Clark feared I might return to sickness if not cared for immediately.

The men had been caught in the open and were greatly bruised by the hail. Those without hats had bloody cuts on their scalps. Others rubbed arms nearly broken. One man, knocked down three times by the hail, almost died before he could crawl beneath the wagon.

Captain Clark, happy we survived the ordeal, was still upset about being trapped in the ravine by the storm water. He lost a rifle, powder horn, and his favorite tomahawk. This did not bother him nearly so much as the loss of the circle with the needle, which points to the star of the north. This the captain used constantly to help him know where we were so he could draw it on his map for Chief Jefferson. He had others, but none so large as this one.

I, too, felt the loss of your cradleboard, for it had been the gift of Otter Woman when we began our journey. I would replace it when we reached The People.

In the morning Captain Clark sent two men back to the ravine to see if they could find any of the lost items. Captain Clark was pleased they found his compass, although it had been buried in mud. Your cradleboard was over the falls, as we would have been had not Captain Clark rescued us. The men said great boulders now filled the ravine where we had been hiding from the storm.

The rain made the ground too slippery for any travel. I sewed you new clothes from a softened deerskin. I wished to fish, but the river had risen overnight more than my own height and the water was running too swift and muddy for fish to bite.

The next day we completed our journey to the White Bear Island camp. The mosquitoes had returned after the storm and tormented us. You smelled like bear, as I had smeared so much bear fat on you to keep off the mosquitoes. We saw many bears in the distance as well as the most buffalo I had ever seen in my life. I thought how much my father, Strong Bear, and brother, Cameahwait, would have enjoyed hunting these animals.

As we neared the land of my people, my thoughts returned to them more and more. It was as if I was sending my spirit ahead to tell them of my return. I saw my brother preparing for his buffalo hunt. My sisters giggling and gathering berries. I knew if they still lived they would not be as I remembered them. They would be four years older, as was I. When I thought of my mother, I forced her death from my mind and remembered her hands dancing as she wove grass baskets.

One night the men celebrated the birth of their nation. There was much dancing and singing and playing of the fiddle until a thunderstorm broke over us and ended the festivities.

In our lodge that evening Captain Clark signed to me his people were twenty-nine years old. I was puzzled by this, and Papa explained that the Americans had once been under the power of a chief who lived far away across another ocean.

The water above the great falls ran as wide and smooth as a lake. It was clear, so clear I could see the trout swimming near the bottom. I fished until we had enough trout to feed everyone. The fish pleased the men as they had eaten so much buffalo and elk that the change was welcome.

Captain Lewis was happy with the three barrels of

bear fat Papa had rendered from the bears. I saved a pouch full for mosquito protection and Papa kept some back to fry his *boudin blanc*. With so many bears around us, growling, eating, and fighting, we did not fear running out of fat. That night the bears surrounded our camp as if they were an enemy tribe preparing for an attack. Seaman patrolled the edges of the camp barking and keeping them at bay.

Captain Lewis wanted to get his metal boat into the water. The metal pieces looked like the skeleton of some strange dream creature as it rested on the shore. He sent the best hunters out for buffalo, as we needed the meat to eat, to mix with bear fat and berries to make pemmican, and for skins to keep our supplies dry in the canoes. The rest of the men began sewing together the elk skins. They used large needles, for the skins had not been properly softened and were tough.

When three skins were together, a few men attached the skins to the boat. The pieces were fitted like the separate skins of a tipi. The stitches were sealed with bear fat and charcoal. Captain Lewis wanted the sticky pitch of the pine tree, but no such trees grew anywhere near our camp.

The strange boat was turned over and fires built beneath it to dry the skins and make them tight. When all was ready, the boat was placed in the water with great ceremony.

Many were the shouts of joy when it floated.

Captain Lewis was extremely pleased, for the metal boat was his idea. The men had carried its heavy frame all the way from Saint Louis.

At dawn, Captain Lewis found his metal boat underwater. The stitches had opened and water filled the boat.

My heart sank, too, for this meant more days before we could finish our journey to the mountains.

20

Captain Lewis wasted little time worrying about his sunken boat. The captains decided they would build two wooden canoes instead. The next day Captain Clark and ten men went to cut down cottonwood trees and fashion the canoes.

The men remaining behind dug another cache, this time for the metal boat.

Although I was eager to continue, I knew we must wait. I rested to regain my strength. For the first time Captain Lewis fished with me, and he was pleased with his catch. We watched otters dive and play. We had not seen many before as the river had been so muddy. Now it ran as clear as the three rivers of the mountains.

We saw eagles flying swiftly to the water and snatching trout. Kingfishers dipped into the water to catch minnows. Curlews swooped down to feast upon grasshoppers. Never before had the mosquitoes been so bad. Clouds of black gnats swarmed into our eyes and mouths. Again, I smeared bear fat on you and tied a handkerchief over your face. It did little good.

The hunters were busy, for I had signed to Captain Lewis we would not find meat so plentiful as we did here. I had Papa explain this was why the Shoshoni moved out of the mountains when buffalo were plentiful.

I watched all the meat the men ate. We roasted four deer one day. The next day we ate an elk and a deer. The following day a bull buffalo.

When the work was completed, the men took the canoes up the river to meet Captain Clark. Captain Lewis and I walked overland to Captain Clark's camp. There we found the two new canoes almost finished. Papa and the other men arrived from the camp downstream. The men were pleased to be together again. But there was no dancing or fiddle playing that evening as all our time was spent preparing for the journey in the morning. A moon had passed since we first reached the great falls. All were eager to go west as soon as possible.

In the morning we set out, two large canoes and six smaller ones. I was happy to be moving once more along the river. Sunflowers bloomed, their yellow heads bobbing in the breeze. I was reminded of the ground meal Bright Morning made from the sunflower seeds. This was especially good when mixed with buffalo marrow and eaten as small cakes. Red, black, yellow, and purple currants grew everywhere, and I picked as many as I could. Captain Lewis especially enjoyed the yellow currants, which he signed were better than those he ate in his own home. Many berries I would dry to mix with buffalo meat and fat to make more pemmican for the captains' journey across the mountains. Although you and I were not traveling with them, my heart and hands wished to make them a gift of much food.

I knew little of what lay beyond the mountains. I remembered one person, named Silver Waters, had crossed them. He told us they were very steep mountains and only a narrow trail led across them. There was little game to be hunted as the mountains were so high and snow remained on them through the summer. On the far side there lived other Shoshoni, different from my band, who ate great numbers of fish and camas roots.

I wondered what it would be like to see the great salt lake of which the captains spoke. Whenever they did, their eyes shone like stars. But even more than I wanted to see the ocean, I wanted to be with The People. When I reached them, even though Papa was my husband and I should obey him, I planned to run away into the mountains with you and hide until the captains left and he left, too.

I told the captains we were nearing the lands of The People. They were eager, for they needed Shoshoni horses to journey over the mountains, especially as they wished to do so before Coldmaker returned.

After three days Captain Clark and two men walked ahead over the land. The captains did not wish to frighten any of The People nearby. They feared the firing of their guns would make the Shoshoni think their Blackfeet and Hidatsa enemies were approaching. I knew this to be true. We always fled to the safety of the mountains when we heard the guns of our enemies. Our tribe had no guns. Our only defense was to flee.

I wished to walk with Captain Clark, but he signed that I should stay with Captain Lewis. He would hurry to find my people, and I could rejoin them sooner if he found The People quickly.

The river ran clear and cold. The mountains at one place came down to the water. All was in shadow, so tall the rocks stood. The men poled and pulled us until we reached the other side and the sun shone upon us again.

Here the land opened. Captain Lewis was disappointed. Ahead we saw only towering mountains tipped with snow. He had hoped no such mountains stood in his path.

I was pleased, for these were the mountains of my home. I strained my eyes for any sign of The People.

We had been traveling for much of the morning when York shouted and pointed ahead. A tall column of smoke rose toward the sky.

Captain Lewis signed to me asking what this meant, but I think he already knew the answer. When

The People were threatened by an enemy, the prairie was set on fire. The smoke warned the tribe to return to the mountains and hide.

Captain Lewis was upset by this. I signed to him these were probably my people and once they saw me, he could get his horses. Still, he was agitated. He ordered the men on. I marveled at him. No matter how many times things became difficult for him, he let his anger melt away and kept pushing forward.

The next day the mountains crowded to the water. The men grew weary of pulling the canoes as they trudged in the cold water.

Then all at once joy burst through me.

I grabbed Papa and said, "This is my home. The People camp here in the early summer to dig the white earth to make paint. This is near to where I was captured. In five suns we will reach the place where the three rivers join to become one."

Papa let out a roar, which echoed up the river. Word soon spread and the men began shouting. Captain Lewis tried to quiet them, but they would not. They were tired of the river and could not wait to cross the mountains.

We found Captain Clark camped beside the river. He had rested all day, such was his pain from the prickly pear needles in his feet. Captain Lewis, his medicines at hand, washed and tended to Captain Clark's feet.

The captains talked long into the night. As always they were friends, but for the first time, Captain Clark's voice rose and he became insistent about something.

In the morning I found out that, even though his feet were blistered and bloody from the cactus spines, Captain Clark was determined to walk ahead and meet The People. Papa was chosen to go with him. I wished to go. Captain Clark signed no to me. Papa explained he wished me to regain all of my strength from the illness, so I could speak well when we met the Shoshoni and began trading for their horses.

Before they left I taught Captain Clark to say the Shoshoni word *Tab-ba-bone*. The word sounded awkward on his tongue. *Tab-ba-bone* meant "stranger," but it was the only word I could think of. The People had no word for white man, for they had never seen one before.

Papa and Captain Clark set off. The men returned to their poles with eagerness. But our three enemies, the mosquitoes, gnats, and prickly pears, still attacked us at every turn. The days grew hot and the men grew even more exhausted. Captain Lewis now poled a canoe to help.

I held you close and told you the Shoshoni names for all we saw: eagles, otters, cranes, beaver, ducks with red breasts, curlews, and snakes.

Seaman journeyed with us and he was the first to

find the needle grass. I had forgotten this sharp bladed grass with a stem as strong as steel. He yelped with pain as he stepped on the grass. The pointed grass stabbed through the men's moccasins and leather leggings. Seaman, his feet bleeding and raw, had to ride in the canoe with us when we encountered needle grass.

Two suns after Captain Clark left us, we saw Papa sitting by the river. Captain Clark had sent him to tell us to continue upstream, although he had not yet met any Shoshoni. I could tell from the look in the men's eyes they were most disappointed, as they had hoped their torture along the river was to end.

Then, two suns later, we poled around a bend. From the south side a river flowed to join us. Ahead, a river from the north shared its waters with ours.

We had at last reached the Three Forks.

My heart soared. Soon I would rejoin The People. My heart was heavy, too, for this was the place where I had been captured. Here my mother, Bright Morning, had died. Did my tribe still live near? What if The People had all moved elsewhere, deep into the mountains? Would I never see them again? What would happen to the captains and their men? Would they stay over the winter or return to their own lands? I tried to keep these thoughts from my mind, but they would not be still.

Captain Lewis ordered the men to make camp while he explored the three rivers. That same afternoon

Captain Clark staggered into camp, his head hot with fever. I ground willow bark for a hot drink. Captain Lewis gave him his medicines and bathed his feet. Through the night, when I awoke to care for you, Pomp, I could hear Captain Clark's heavy breathing.

In the morning Captain Clark felt better, but the captains decided to stay in this camp until the men's strength returned. While they rested the men dried their equipment and mended their moccasins and leggings ripped by cactus. The best hunters hunted while Captain Lewis continued his explorations.

I took you, Pomp, on a long walk that first morning. I wished to find any sign The People had returned here since we were attacked by the Hidatsa. I told you of how Antelope and I had first seen the Hidatsa approaching. I told you how we had scattered like rabbits and that Antelope jumped through the stream and I fell. I told you how I was captured and taken to the village of the Hidatsa and later became wife to Papa. You were too young to understand these things, yet I felt I must share them with you at this place where I was torn from my people.

I told you how life is a circle. The sun, moon, stars, and seasons travel in a circle. The People make tipis in circles. The circle of my life had come back to where I was born. Now you were part of my circle and would learn ways of the Shoshoni.

At camp I worried for the health of Captain Clark.

With York's help I gathered more willow bark and made a hot poultice, which I applied to his feet. The heat helped draw out some of the infection, and by afternoon he could hobble around camp.

We stayed here for two days and then proceeded on. Most days you and I went with the canoes. Once I walked with Captain Lewis and showed him the shallow place in the river where I had been captured. The heat beat down on us as the men struggled against the river, which ran fast over slippery rocks and boulders.

Each day one captain ranged far looking for The People. He would return a day or two later with no word of them. Then one afternoon I saw the rock I had been looking for, the rock shaped like the head of a swimming beaver.

"Har-na-Hap-pap! *Beaverhead Rock,*" shouted *Pomp.*

I signed to Captain Clark I knew this place. My people should be near.

The men grew excited and wished to leave the canoes, make packs for their backs, and set off to find the Shoshoni. The captains, although eager to reach The People, decided against this, as they needed the goods in the bundles to trade for horses.

Thus it was Captain Lewis who decided he must find the Shoshoni without any further delay. With only three men he set forth as we struggled up the river.

Days passed with no word from Captain Lewis. I ached to get out of the canoe and walk, but Captain Clark would not allow this. Day after day we battled our way up the river, each day more difficult than the one before.

A half a moon had passed when suddenly Drouillard ran into our camp. With him was an Indian, a Shoshoni warrior!

Immediately, Captain Clark sent the warrior back to tell Captain Lewis he was near. He called for Papa and me to come with him, for The People had been found.

My blood rushed through me like the spring melt-water as we walked. I willed my feet not to run, but they almost refused to obey me. Ahead lay my family. My father. My brother. My sisters. If they still lived.

We broke out of the trees and there was Captain Lewis wearing a Shoshoni robe of otter skins. Beside him stood a Shoshoni chief with Captain Lewis's fur hat upon his head. A group of warriors was behind them. A few women gathered in the distance.

Captain Clark approached, his palms held outward, the sign of Shoshoni friendship I had taught him. The chief came up to him, hugged him in the Shoshoni way, and draped strings of shells in his hair, a Shoshoni welcome gift. All the warriors hugged Captain Clark and there was much excitement.

I stood in the shadows, not daring to move for fear

that my dream, so long wished for, was not real. Then I heard a shout. A woman leaped toward me and hugged me.

She said my Shoshoni name again and again until I knew her to be my friend Antelope. I had never known if she lived to return to The People after her escape.

"Antelope!" I cried.

She laughed. "Now I am called Jumping Fish for the way I jumped through the stream when we ran from the Hidatsa."

We laughed and cried and laughed again. She took you from my arms and held you up high. You giggled and tugged her hair.

I tried to talk, but the words did not flow. I had not spoken the Shoshoni tongue in such a long time, only a few words to you, Pomp. But as I listened to Jumping Fish the words returned in a flood.

Before we could share our stories and I could ask about my family, the captains ordered camp to be made and a sail tied between trees to give them shade.

I was called forth with Papa and a man called Labiche. Together we were to talk with the chief and trade for the horses the captains were determined to have.

Jumping Fish held on to you, Pomp, outside the circle of men.

I licked my lips and willed my heart to slow. If the

captains got their horses, maybe Papa would let me live with my people. I bowed my head before the men and took a deep breath. I knew I had to ask the chief for as many horses as there are fingers on ten hands.

I raised my eyes and looked into eyes of the chief. My voice froze in my throat.

Cameahwait, my brother!

I ran to him and in the way of our people, drew a blanket over our heads. Beneath it we cried our joy at being reunited.

W hat did my uncle look like?" Pomp asked.
"He was tall like Captain Lewis and had big
shoulders like York. His eyes sparkled like Papa's do when
he makes an especially good trade. The People looked to
his wisdom to guide them. He told me he wished for us to
stay with him and he would teach you the ways of the
Shoshoni as a good uncle should."

"Why didn't we stay?" queried Pomp.

"That lies in the next part of our story," said
Sacagawea. "The part I tell now."

She took a deep breath before beginning.

I fought back my tears as I interpreted for the captains. Even so they burst through like a weak place in
a beaver's dam, such was my joy of seeing my brother
once again.

I told Cameahwait the white men had not brought
guns to trade now, but if The People provided them
with horses, the guns would come later. Then they
could protect themselves from the Blackfeet and
Hidatsa. I explained the captains sought the horses to

cross the mountains.

Your uncle told me to tell the captains he would wait for the guns. He said he would urge his people to trade their horses to the captains.

The captains were pleased to learn this and they gave many presents to my people. My brother received a medal with a likeness of the white chief Jefferson on it. They gave him also a blue coat, red leggings, a knife, a handkerchief, and tobacco for my brother's pipe. They gave paint, knives, beads of many colors, mirrors, and many other things to the rest of the Shoshoni.

By now York, Seaman, and the rest of the men had caught up to us. My people were shy of York at first until I told him how he was a great hunter who could also erect a tipi. The woman laughed at this, but I told them it was so. They marveled at Seaman for no Shoshoni dog was so large nor could hunt so well.

As the sun set, the hunters brought in four deer. We feasted, laughed, cried, and talked long into the night. Even in our tipi the captains continued talking, making plans for tomorrow, plans which took me to the village of my people. This I did not know until the sun rose. Sleep came hard for me because my brother had told me only he was left of my family. My father and sisters had died at the hands of our enemies.

All I had longed for these many years was gone as if smoke in the wind. What was I to do now? I had you, Papa, and my brother. I did not know which trail to follow anymore. I had followed the trail that brought me home. But where was my home now?

My mind wandered back over the four moons since we had left the fort by the Mandan. In that time I had cared for you, found food for the men, helped the captains with many camp chores, taken care of the sick, and been cared for myself. The captains were like brothers to me.

Was I to leave them now that I had returned to the mountains? Only the Great Spirit knew.

In the morning Captain Clark, Papa, York, and I joined ten men who went with Cameahwait to the Shoshoni village. Jumping Fish walked beside me, her tongue never still. I told her my story of what had happened after her escape and how I came to be with the captains. She asked me many questions about them and I shared the wonders that I had seen as I had traveled with them. For much of the walk she carried you, Pomp, the first time anyone else carried you since we left Fort Mandan.

My heart was heavy when we reached the village of my people. Heavy for my family who had joined their ancestors, but heavy, too, for the hunger I saw on their skintight faces and shrunken bellies. With the captains we had eaten well most days. The hunters were good and the game plentiful. The People had but three old guns, so they could not shoot much game. What they shot did little to fill so many empty bellies.

The tribe had grown since I was captured. There were one hundred warriors and three times as many women and children. As was our way, even when hungry, The People were cheerful. A successful buffalo hunt would hold the wolf of hunger at bay.

The men were preparing for the hunt, and soon The People would travel to the buffalo lands to end their hunger. They waited in their mountain hideaway. Only a moon earlier the dreaded Blackfeet had attacked their village. They had escaped with only few lives lost. Most of their horses were saved.

One more surprise awaited me. I met White Bear, to whom I had been promised as his wife when I was a child. He had two fine wives and many children now, and as I was Papa's wife, he no longer desired me to be his wife. This pleased me, for I did not wish two husbands.

As a warrior wrestles a bear trying to kill him, so I wrestled my thoughts. I had wanted to be with The People, to raise you as Shoshoni. But now I saw how desperate they were and how great their suffering. I did not want you to starve. I knew we could not remain with them.

All at once, like flame bursting from a birch log, I knew we would travel with the captains, my new brothers. Like them we would journey to the great lake of salt water.

I told Jumping Fish my plan. At first she was silent, then she wept. She wished for me to stay, but I would not. I consoled her, telling her the captains might return this way and we would be together again. After that, I knew not what I would do. In any case, I reminded her, I must do as my husband ordered.

We stayed only one day with The People, as Captain Clark was eager to explore the mountains for a pass through them. My brother had told him the river was too swift and dangerous for canoes. No man who had ever ventured down this river returned to tell his tale.

Captain Clark, however, must see this for himself. We walked along the river until the captain realized passage was impossible.

We returned to the village where the captain asked my brother to ask his people to help him and Captain Lewis cross the pass with their equipment.

My brother was reluctant. The People had to prepare for their buffalo hunt and move their own village. They were weak with hunger and even a sun's delay meant hardship. Yet with many trade goods, Captain Clark finally got him to agree.

Most of the village, men, women, and children, came to the camp of Captain Lewis to help. Captain Lewis had caught many fish in a net stretched across the river and so there was much to eat, as well as maize and beans, which the captains served. Papa wished we had some fine, fat buffalo for his *boudin blanc* to add to the celebration.

Captain Lewis gave Papa some trade goods, which he gave to the uncle of Jumping Fish for a horse. You squealed with joy as you rode with me for the first time, the bouncing horse making you laugh until you were so tired you slept.

Together, the Shoshoni and the white men began the march over the high mountain pass back to the village. With so many hands and backs to help carry the packs, we made the journey only once. The packs were heavy, and The People hungry, so we did not cross in one day. At the end of the first day's walk, I heard my brother tell his men they would leave the captains in the morning to go down the mountain to begin their buffalo hunt.

I was angered greatly. Cameahwait had promised the captains he would aid them in crossing the pass. Now he was breaking his word.

My heart was torn, for now I must go against my people, the Shoshoni, to help the captains. Was I not Shoshoni? Was I a *Tab-ba-bone?*

I told Papa, who told Captain Lewis what Cameahwait was planning to do. This made the captain angry and he scolded Papa for not telling him sooner. He feared to scold my brother, for then he would not trade the horses we desperately needed. Captain Lewis reminded my brother of his promise. Cameahwait honored his word.

That night frost covered us as we slept. Coldmaker had returned to the mountains. The captains must cross soon or give up their quest and return to their people.

This I knew neither captain would do. Each would fight to his last breath to finish the journey upon which they had started. The medicine of their chief Jefferson was powerful indeed.

When the captains were reunited, they talked much between themselves. I was kept busy with the trading for many more horses. The captains had only traded for ten and needed many more.

Without letting the captains know, I did the best for The People. The captains traded only a coat or a pair of leggings for the first horses. Now, knowing how desperate The People were to be on their hunt and desperate for the goods the captains carried, I urged them to bargain for more goods. I did this, not to go against my new people, but to help my old people.

The price for a horse rose steadily until the Shoshoni were receiving many blankets, coats, beads, knives, and awls for each horse. Captain Clark's face went as red as his hair when he was forced to trade his pistol, a knife, and many bullets and gunpowder for a horse he desired.

My divided heart healed over this. I helped the captains get the horses they needed and helped The People get the things they wanted.

Before the men talked, my brother lit his pipe and held it in the four directions. He bade the captains to remove their moccasins as The People held council with their feet bared. The captains shared the pipe and gave my brother some of their people's tobacco.

My brother drew in the dirt a map for the captains. He made the rivers to the west and placed heaps of sand to show the height of the mountains. My brother said the river cut through the tallest mountains, which never lost their snow and ran through the lands of the People of the Pierced Nose. This river emptied its waters in a big river, which flowed to the lake that tasted bad.

When I translated this for the captains their faces grew great with smiles. This is what they wished to hear. They knew now that once they crossed the Shining Mountains they could make their way to the ocean.

The captains wished to know more about the western country and asked many questions. Then they asked if there was a Shoshoni who could guide them over the mountains.

My brother said yes, Silver Waters. He was old, but he knew the trail to the People of the Pierced Nose. My brother, although chief, could not order Silver Waters to guide the captains. In the Shoshoni way, each man chooses his own life path. But he would ask what Silver Waters wished to be paid. With this, the council ended.

The captains told their men to make a great feast to which all were invited to share.

My brother enjoyed many of the white man's foods, especially the lump of sugar I gave him. Never before had he tasted anything so sweet.

Now the captains had twenty-nine horses and were prepared to cross the peaks of the Shining Mountains.

In the morning I hugged Jumping Fish good-bye as well as my brother. I told them we would meet again the next year when the captains returned this way. In my brother's eyes, however, I saw sadness, for he thought he would never see me again in this world.

Old Toby is what the captains called our guide Silver Waters. To them his Shoshoni name sounded as such. We left at dawn, before the frost melted, with our things in packs on the horses' backs. Our journey was to the north and up. We had to cross another pass that would lead us to the western waters.

Three suns rose and fell before we reached the pass. The rocky trail was difficult to walk on. Low hanging trees blocked our path, and the men swung their axes to clear a way for the horses. The mountains rose high above us, blocking out the sun for most of the day. We climbed and climbed, slowly. Off to one side the earth dropped steeply to a river far below. The men held the horses' reins tightly, but not wrapped around their hands. Often the horses slipped, but none fell over the cliff. If a man was then fastened to his animal, he would fall to his death.

As my brother had warned, there was no game to be hunted. The buffalo, elk, antelope, and sheep lived toward where the sun rose. We ate a few grouse, but these did little to ease the men's great hunger. On the second night out the men ate the last of the salt pork they had brought with them.

The third night snow fell, and the captains cast worried glances at the mountains towering above them. To be caught without food in a heavy snowfall might mean death. I worried for you, Pomp, although you still drank of my milk. If my sickness returned, I worried about who would care for you. Maybe I should have left you with your uncle, I thought, but I could not bear to be parted from you.

"I would like to have lived with him," Pomp said solemnly. "But if I did so, then we would not be on this journey to Captain Clark. Is he my new uncle?"

Sacagawea paused while she thought about this.

"Yes, it is so. Captain Clark is a brother to me. Now he will be your uncle and teach you the ways of his people. I hope someday you will go west to greet your other uncle, Cameahwait."

"I promise," Pomp pledged.

"I hope the Great Spirit allows you to do so," Sacagawea said before she continued.

We crossed the pass and began descending the slope to a silver river flowing north. The horses whinnied, for the snow-covered trail was steep and the footing unsure.

One horse slipped and rolled down the steep slope. A tree stopped his fall. I held my breath, certain the horse could not have survived a fall onto the broken, jagged rocks. Captain Lewis scrambled down to it. When the crushed load was lifted from its back, the horse rose onto its feet. Soon it rejoined the others, ready to proceed. Looking down the hill, Captain Lewis's face showed that he was as amazed as I was that the animal was unharmed by its misadventure.

Late in the afternoon we reached the bottom and found a village as large as The People's. Captain Clark called me forward to talk with these people, but they were not Shoshoni. They called themselves Salish. A Shoshoni boy who lived among them spoke their tongue. In Shoshoni words he told me what they said. I told it in Hidatsa to Papa, who told it in the French tongue to Labiche, who explained their words to the captains. I am sure much was mistaken in this way of speaking, because for so many to tell things the same way is difficult.

These people knew Old Toby and claimed friendship with The People. They themselves were preparing to climb the trail to join my brother, Cameahwait, in his buffalo hunt on the plains.

The Salish people had not much food, only berries and roots. These they shared with us. They were also willing to trade thirteen horses to the captains. Now we had horses enough to continue as well as three colts too young to leave their mothers.

The captains ordered the equipment to be divided among all the horses. With farewells shouted, we continued north while the Salish rode east.

Food remained scarce. Two grouse we ate and a few berries still clinging to their bushes. The captains had metal cans with soup in them, but would not open them until they had to.

We followed the river for three days. Silver Waters had me tell the captains this is where we must leave the river and cross west to the tallest of the mountains. He also had me tell the captains if we continued on the river it would lead us to a pass, which was easily crossed back to the Missouri. He said we were only four days' horse ride from that river.

Captain Lewis's eyes flared with anger, for we had spent two moons reaching this place, which could have been reached in four suns. But his anger died out quickly and he ordered the men to prepare to climb the mountains.

He sent out all the hunters who returned with four deer and a beaver, enough food for one day.

One hunter returned with three Pierced Nose Indians. Through sign talk the captains learned only five sleeps were necessary to cross the mountains to a great river, which would carry us to the lake of the ill-tasting water. One man also offered to guide the captains to his people across the mountains.

That night some horses strayed and much time was spent finding them. The Pierced Nose man strayed, too, and when we were ready to depart, he was not to be found. Old Toby assured the captains he knew the way and so we continued.

Long was the trail and great was our hunger. Snow fell, as did rain and hail. Then Old Toby told the captains he was lost. He had missed a turn in the trail and we must go a different way.

The men were as tired as the horses. A sadness entered the camp such as I had never seen, not even when the metal boat sank. To ease our hunger the captains ordered a colt killed for meat. I ate none, although my belly growled.

Snow fell, covering the trail and soaking our moccasins. Lumps of snow dropped off the branches as we passed, soaking our clothes. Hunger was with us and each evening we killed a colt. Starved, I ate of the meat, for I feared for my health and your needs. Never before had I been so cold, so hungry, so weary even my bones ached.

The horses' ribs shown through their hides, for there was no grass for them to eat. The captains talked late into the night and decided to split into two groups. Captain Clark would take a small group ahead to hunt. We would follow his route across the mountains.

We ate the last soup in the cans, mixed with a little bear fat and the tallow of candles. With this meager meal our food was gone.

After that we ate a coyote, and a few crayfish from a stream and a grouse. Captain Lewis urged us on, not letting us rest except when necessary. Captain Clark had poor hunting, only a scrawny horse he found, for there was no game high in the mountains. He left horsemeat by the trail, which served to take the bite out of our hunger but not end it.

Still we marched until we saw below us a flat plain. In climbing down to it we met a man whom Captain Clark had sent back with fish and roots. He told us a village of the Pierced Nose People lay ahead.

When we reached the village Captain Clark and his men greeted us warmly as did the Pierced Nose People. They had many salmon fish, which they shared. They also shared the roots of the camas plant. We ate greedily, for our hunger was great.

I fear this was a mistake. Every one of us grew ill from too much fish and camas. Seven suns would pass before our health returned.

During this time, although sick, the captains talked with Twisted Hair, the chief of the Pierced Nose. On a white elk skin, he drew a map of the rivers the captains should follow to reach the Columbia, the great river that flowed to the salt lake. He signed that in five sleeps we would reach this river, and five sleeps more would find us at the great falls of the Columbia.

Little was done for a week as the men were too ill. The captains gave them many medicines, but they did no good. Captain Lewis grew so sick he lay for days in the shade.

The captains and the men looked back often at the Shining Mountains behind us. Coldmaker had not trapped us there and no men had been lost. I marveled at the men's cheerfulness, for as great as their hardship had been, they still followed the captains with trust.

Among the Pierced Nose People lived a woman named Watkuweis, a name meaning "Returned from a Far Country." Like me, she had been captured. Her Blackfeet captors had badly mistreated her. She had then lived with a white trader who was kind to her and saved her life so she could return to the Pierced Nose People.

Through signs she told me the Pierced Nose People had planned to kill the captains and their men to possess their guns, bullets, and wealth. She persuaded them not to do this, as one of the men was the same who had protected her from the Blackfeet.

This I knew not to be true, but in telling this lie, she saved the captains and their men from death. I hugged her hard in the Shoshoni way.

As their strength returned the men grew excited. They cut down trees and made canoes, for the end of their journey lay less than a moon ahead.

Captain Lewis took many days to regain his health, but at last he did. The canoes were placed in the river and loaded.

The Pierced Nose People promised to care for their horses until we returned the next year. It was here I learned the captains thought they might not come this way again. They hoped to find a great ship at the ocean, a ship that would carry them back to their people without having to cross any more mountains.

Our spirits soared as the canoes sped down the river. The men rested, having little to do except steer as the river swiftly carried us. We reached a place where the river filled with rocks. Eager to proceed, the men took the canoes through the rapids, wetting themselves and their gear but determined to move on.

Old Toby disappeared one night. The captains had not even been able to pay him for guiding them. I was sad, for without his help we would have perished in the mountains. Yet I understood better than any others his desire to return to The People.

One night we camped with a small group of the Pierced Nose People, who were willing to share with us their fish and roots. The captains refused, knowing this diet had made the men so ill. Instead, they traded for many fat dogs, which the men ate with much pleasure. Only Captain Clark refused to eat the dogs and hunted ducks for his meals.

We stayed with the river, passing many Indian villages on the shores. Some nights we camped with these people, trading for food. Not wanting to waste time hunting, the men continued trading for dogs.

Each night there was dancing and Monsieur Cruzatte played his fiddle with much enthusiasm. The Americans danced their dances and the Pierced Nose People danced theirs. York danced with you in his arms, both of you laughing.

Our river joined the Columbia and the excitement grew even more, for the Columbia ran to the salt water.

Even the difficulties we faced on this river brought no sorrow to the men. We shot down rapids and portaged around waterfalls. But each evening's camp brought us closer to the end.

We no longer had mosquitoes and gnats to plague us, but their cousins, the fleas, swarmed into our hair and clothes, biting us with a viciousness we had never experienced before. Seaman scratched as much as we did.

At one place the river narrowed and the water rose and plunged more than any we had seen before. The riverbanks were too high to carry the canoes, and so they must be paddled through. The captains sent the men who could not swim along the shore with the guns, books, and other things that would be lost if the canoes overturned.

Hundreds of the Pierced Nose People stood along the shore below this rapid, holding long poles to fish equipment from the river. They were certain no canoe could survive the tumbling water. I walked with you and Papa along the shore. The canoes began their journey. The river tossed them, and for many long moments they disappeared in the spray of water. Cheers roared from the Americans and the Indians as the canoes shot through without accident.

Below these falls we met with people who lived in houses made of wood. They had salmon dried on racks, for the salmon are many in the Columbia below this place. These people called themselves Chinook and they were at war with the Pierced Nose People. The captains hoped to bring peace between these tribes and offered the Chinook trade if they would not fight the Pierced Nose. To this they agreed.

The river continued to flow swiftly, and the men pushed on, halting only to trade for fish. At last the rapid waters ceased and we had entered a new land.

I dipped my finger into the water to see if it tasted like salt. I touched a drip to your tongue, too. The water was fresh, but the captains were pleased, for the river rose and fell each day just as if one would fill and empty a bowl. Papa explained to me this is what the ocean did twice a day, and this meant we were very close to it.

Along the river, trees of a kind I had never seen before towered to the sky. Much bigger than the trees you see now on that bank of the Missouri.

She pointed to the thick forests they were passing through.

Of these trees the Chinook built their canoes and homes. Geese and ducks were plentiful. We ate well. Many were the Indian villages we passed, for the captains did not wish to spare more time. Winter was stalking us, and we needed to find a place to winter over as the captains had done at the village of the Mandan.

Clouds of fog covered the river, so we could not see our way. We spent many days in camp until past noon. This frustrated the men and the captains. I did not mind, for I had chores to do and you to care for.

Many Chinook visited the captains and traded with them. The captains were not pleased with their trades. The Chinook asked much in return from the captains for fish and other foods.

Each morning I tasted the water and found it different in flavor. Soon it tasted much with salt and made you pucker your lips when I touched my finger to your mouth.

Rain fell often, but this did not dampen the men's spirits. Each day we met more Indians. Although they did not speak the same hand sign talk the people east of the mountains did, we understood enough to trade.

Many Chinook paddled their great canoes to greet us. One had the head of a great brown bear carved on it. Another had an open-mouthed salmon. Many had the faces of men carved on them.

The Chinook traded otter furs to the captains. This pleased them. These Indians also wore many clothes of the white men: coats, shirts, and hats. They wore blankets of red and blue stripes. They had pistols and steel axes. This, too, pleased the captains, for it meant they traded with other white men and that the ocean must be very near.

One morning we awoke to fog sprinkled with rain. The fog lifted a little and we set out. It was as if we were in a swirling smoke. Then suddenly the fog disappeared and the blue sky appeared.

Captain Clark roared.

"Ocean in view!"

Far away I heard another roar like unending thunder. This I learned to be waves taller than a man, breaking onto rocks, waves of the saltwater ocean.

Rain fell too heavy and hard that night for us to celebrate. Instead we huddled beneath our robes, trying to stay dry. Yet every man's eyes sparkled like dew on the grass, for they had accomplished what they had set out to do.

chapter 22

Our joy turned to sorrow in the morning. The captains discovered we had not truly reached the saltwater ocean. Instead the river was wide and great with waves, which tossed our canoes as if they were twigs hurling through rapid waters. Our canoe rose and fell so much my stomach grew sick and the world whirled around. I could not lie down in the bottom of the canoe for all the water splashed in by the waves. No food could I keep down, for my stomach leaped to my throat. The tossing waters seemed like a game to you.

Rain. Rain. And more rain. Never before had I seen the sky let loose its tears as much. In the mountains and on the prairie we had many storms, the kind you know, which blow up, drop their waters, and move on. Not so in this land, for there the rain is like a wet blanket, soaking you always. When the rain does not fall, then the fog covers you with its dampness. Fires became hard to light and dry wood almost impossible to find.

We had brought fish with us from the Chinook People, but it soon spoiled in the wet. The deerskin clothes on our backs ripped open from rot. The few fires started gave off little heat but much smoke, for the wood was so wet. The high waters carried with them huge trees, which crashed upon the shore, tossed onto the rocks like you would toss a stick. The rain loosened rocks on the cliffs and they rolled down upon us night and day. Strong winds toppled even the giant trees, which sometimes fell near our camp.

Each day the captains searched for a way to safely reach the ocean and get out of the leaping river waves. But the wind and waves were too strong for the men.

For many days we remained on the north shore, unable to paddle forward, unable to climb the steep cliffs and get away from the river, unable to cross to the south shore over the open water.

I wondered why the captains had come so far and endured so many dangers to reach such a miserable place. I had wished to see the ocean, but now I wished to turn back to the mountains. Even the crossing of the Shining Mountains was better than the unpleasantness of this place.

Luckily, we had food. The Clatsop People living on the south bank of the river crossed to us in their broad, light canoes, which they made for these waters. Our heavy log canoes looked pitiful beside theirs.

The captains sent three men with the Clatsop to

find a better place for us to camp. One returned to tell us of a sandy place protected from the wind with much driftwood and game.

Captain Lewis, Seaman, and five men went ahead to this place. Captain Lewis wished also to see the true ocean and to find the white men who had traveled there in great canoes upon the ocean.

We remained in the camp with Captain Clark, packing our things and preparing to leave when the winds lessened.

We moved to this sheltered beach and stayed for more days while the captains explored. The hunters brought in a few lean deer. York shot many geese and ducks. I dug wappato, a root, which the Chinook had shown me where to find. These I cooked in their skins. Some men caught fish. We drank only the rainwater, for the river was far too salty. We did not starve.

Captain Clark asked Papa and some men to join him to journey to the ocean. I wished to go with them. It was my desire now to see the salt water. But the route was too rugged for me to carry you on my back, so I remained in camp with the men who said they could see enough of the salt water right where they were. If we remained here for the winter, I would walk to the ocean, I told myself, and we would both look upon its waters.

The captains were eager to leave this miserable place. They had still hoped to meet other white men by this shore. The Clatsop and Chinook had told them white men came there to trade, but none were there now.

Many times these people came to us to trade fish and wappato for the things the men had. They also brought beautiful otter skins of the kind that swim in the ocean. This excited the captains, for their chief Jefferson wished to know of these animals and their numbers just as he had wished to know of the beaver and buffalo.

One man had an otter-skin robe, which Captain Clark desired. The captain offered him many axes, awls, and knives in exchange for it but the man would not trade. He wished only for blue beads, but these the captains had very few remaining. The man pointed to the belt of blue beads, which I wore at my waist. These I had treasured since the day Captain Clark had given them to me as a gift so long ago at Fort Mandan. You loved to run your little fingers over these beads as blue as the summer sky.

I unfastened the belt and offered it to the man for his otter-skin robe. He took the beads and gave me the robe, which I gave to Captain Clark. Much I owed to both captains, but to Captain Clark especially for his many kindnesses to me and you, and for the time he saved our lives when the flood waters trapped us in the ravine.

Captain Clark signed me to come with him. He

went to a large bundle covered with a deer skin to keep off the rain. He opened the bundle and withdrew a coat.

"Can you guess the color of the coat?"

"As blue as the summer sky?"

"Yes . . ."

The captains decided we must spend the winter somewhere near. Hunters who had gone to the south side of the river returned saying there was a place with plenty of trees, little wind, and the tracks of many, many elk.

The captains asked each man if they wished to remain at this place or cross to the south side. York and myself were asked our wishes, too. Like York, I wanted to cross over. I signed I wished a place where many wappatoes grew. I had a liking for them, as did many of the men.

Captain Clark laughed at this and wrote it in his book as he did after questioning each man.

We decided to cross and winter on the south side of the Columbia.

"Did you see the ocean?" Pomp asked.

"Not yet, but soon," she answered.

chapter 23

We rounded a point of land and paddled to a stream leading to where Captain Lewis wished to build the fort.

The place was on a low hill by a stream. Around the hill were many swamps where the hunters found elk signs. The forest was thick and the men spent many days cutting down trees to clear a space for the fort.

The men built small log cabins together with a wall of pointed logs around them. For the roof they split logs into long boards, which kept out the constant rain. In the center of the fort was an open place where the men met and worked.

The captains shared one cabin. In it the log cutters left a tree stump so large Captain Clark used it for a table. You, Papa, and I lived in another cabin. The rest of the men shared three cabins. A room was for storing food, one for smoking elk meat, and one where the men received their orders for each day.

We still carried the buffalo-skin tipi although it leaked terribly. It, like our clothes, had begun to rot from the rain and damp. I spent much time over the winter repairing it with elk skin so we could use it on our return to the Shining Mountains. For this I knew we would do.

The captains, knowing no ship would come for them or even be in these waters to trade with them for supplies for the return home, began planning to leave. We must spend the winter here, which although wet, was not bitter cold.

Captain Lewis often entertained visiting Clatsop People who came to trade wappatoes and fish for beads, knives, and fishhooks. Chief among them was Coboway. He liked the captains and signed to them the best places to hunt elk and catch fish. To honor his tribe the captains named this wintering place Fort Clatsop.

Three weeks passed before the fort was finished. As soon as the walls were up we moved into our room, although it did not yet have a roof. Soon the roof was on, and for the first time in a moon we were out of the rain.

One morning the men woke the captains with shots from their guns and with much shouting and singing. The celebration of Christmas had come again. I ran my hand over my waist where the blue-beaded belt had hung for so long, remembering when Captain Clark had given it to me. The captains were pleased with the men's actions and there were many smiles and excited talking. The men gave each other gifts of moc-casins, clothes, and things they had traded from the Indians we had met on our journey.

I was eager to give, too, for I had gotten for Captain Clark many white weasel tails from my brother. These I had carried and kept dry as a gift to him. My heart still warms when I think of the pleasure my gift gave him.

The captains gave tobacco to the men and hand-kerchiefs for those who did not smoke. We ate a meal of elk, boiled fish, and fresh water. We did not eat so well as we had the Christmas the year before, but the men were cheerful and enjoyed themselves with music and dancing in their rooms. The rain fell too hard for us to be outside.

It was on this day you took your first steps. Captain Clark held your hands and then let you go. You took three short steps and tumbled onto the ground. You held your arms out for him to do it again. Each time you took more steps until you could toddle from man to man.

Papa told me the men missed their families far away, and our family made them feel less sick for their homes.

That night I thought about Papa's words. I knew my people now were the captains and their men. I was Shoshoni. I was Hidatsa. I was American.

How three peoples could be in one I did not

understand. You are of three peoples, too. Shoshoni. French. American. I pondered this as I fell asleep.

"What am I now?" Pomp asked.

"You are still the same. Yet who knows what your life circle will bring. You could become something else, as I did."

The next day Captain Clark took some men to camp by the ocean where they would boil the salt water for salt for our food. I longed to visit but stayed behind to cook, make moccasins, and care for you. When the weather was better, I would join them, as I had yet to see the ocean, although we could hear it pounding the shore.

My journey to the ocean happened sooner than I expected. The Clatsop brought word of a great fish, which had been found by the water. This fish was longer than our fort and as wide as one of the cabins. At first I believed we did not understand the hand signs of the Clatsop, but the captains had heard of such large fish before. They called it a whale, and were determined to gather its meat for us to eat.

Captain Clark took two canoes and enough men to paddle them. I had not yet seen the ocean and desired to do so. I must also see the great fish with my own eyes, for not until then would I believe such a creature existed.

I approached Captain Clark with my request, but he refused. I signed to him the many things I had done to help the men, such as find food and trade for horses. I told him I had come all this way and suffered much. I was as determined as he had been to see the great western lake of salt water. I wished to see the great fish, too.

Captain Clark at first said nothing. Then he burst into a smile and said I may go to the whale and I must bring you, Pomp, for to see such a sight comes only once in a man's life.

To reach the ocean we took the trail the men had made through the forest to the shore. This trail they used to travel between the fort and the camp where the salt was made. Many trips were made along this trail, for the men had been without salt for a long time, and it was all we had to flavor the poor elk meat we ate.

At the trail's end, I saw the ocean. My eyes were filled with the sight. It was as if one gazed upon the prairie, an ocean of grass. My ears filled with the pounding of the waves upon the shore. Huge rocks poked up from the water like fat fingers reaching for the sky. Waves crashed against them, showering spray high into the air.

The men at the salt camp were pleased to see us, for theirs was a tiring job with little excitement. They scooped ocean water into five kettles, which bubbled over a fire of driftwood. As the water boiled away, grains of white salt were scraped into baskets. Much wood and water was used to get very little salt.

We stayed the night with the men and in the morning crossed a high mountain to reach the whale fish. The rocks were slippery and we spent our breath climbing. From the top we looked down at the ocean running up in waves over a long, sandy beach. As our breath returned we saw many Indian women loaded with heavy baskets of the meat of the whale fish. Our men were surprised they had made the climb with no appearance of weariness.

But Captain Clark had come too late. The people living there had stripped the whale of all of its fat and meat. All that remained was a skeleton of bones washed by the salty waters. I paced the length of these bones and could scarcely believe what I saw. The animal was twice the length of the fort.

Captain Clark approached the people and traded for many pounds of fat and meat. This we carried back with us to Fort Clatsop, where we used the fat for cooking. The meat we roasted. It did not taste like either the trout or salmon of which we had eaten so much. As I swallowed the meat I could not believe such a creature swam beneath the salt waters. I wondered what other mysteries lay there.

The days at the fort became much the same. Rain fell. The captains wrote in their books and talked much. Captain Clark drew his many maps. I made moccasins of elk hide until my fingers ached. Many of the men did the same. Upon the return journey we must face our enemy the prickly pear cactus again. This time we would be prepared.

We made ten pairs for everyone. I even fashioned moccasins for Seaman, who struggled against me when I placed them on his feet. I knew later he would wear them, however. The men jerked elk meat, repaired rifles, made new clothes, and told the stories of their adventures on our journey.

Often the Clatsop People would visit to watch us and trade. For a handful of fishhooks, the captains bought woven grass hats for all of the men. These were the hats the Clatsop wore. They were shaped like a tipi, and were quite excellent. The rain rolled off them and not down our necks. These we needed because in all the time we spent in Fort Clatsop we saw the sun only for six days.

Captain Lewis traded his best blue coat with gold on the shoulders with Chief Coboway for one of his fast canoes. He wanted another, but did not have enough left to trade for it. All the captains had left to trade fit in two handkerchiefs. Instead, the captains gave their fort to Chief Coboway, even though he would have taken it once we left.

Two moons passed, then a third before the captains felt we were ready to return up the Columbia to cross the Shining Mountains again.

Only once before had I seen the captains take any-thing that belonged to the Indians without trading something in return. That was when they desperately needed dry firewood. Now, however, they took one of Chief Coboway's many canoes and hid it so he could not find it.

At last, late in *Yu'a-Mea'a*, the Warming Moon, we placed the canoes in the water, loaded them, and began the long journey east.

In the rain we began paddling back up the Columbia. The men and the captains were excited. They were returning home after two years' absence. I smiled for them, but in my heart was a heavy sadness.

Where was my home? I wondered.

Would I return to live with the Shoshoni? No, for Papa did not wish to do so.

Would I return to the Mandan village and live there?

Would we travel with the captains to their country?

These thoughts were in my head as the men plunged their paddles into the water.

I looked back to this place where we had lived for the winter. Another part of my life's journey had been added to my circle.

And to yours.

chapter 24

Huckleberry leaves, the size of squirrels' ears, rustled in the wind. I thought of Otter Woman. Leaves this size meant the time to plant maize had returned. In my mind I pictured her digging holes and dropping in the seeds she had saved. I wished her a good crop.

The men fought the waters of the Columbia as they had fought the Missouri. We had come swiftly down the river in the fall, but must now battle the current. The men, rested from their winter at the fort, pushed themselves hard. The captains urged them forward for they wished to reach the Pierced Nose People by *Bu'Hisea-Mea'a,* the Budding Moon. These people had promised to care for the men's horses without which we would have much difficulty crossing the Shining Mountains.

The canoes did not carry much, for we had little left. Gone were the great bundles of trade goods. Gone were the wool clothes and kegs of flour and meat. Gone were the soups, maize, beans, and tobacco. The tattered tents had rotted. Only our tipi remained. We carried the many moccasins the men had made and their new elk-skin clothes. Still, the captains had little fear. They had many bullets and much gunpowder left. They had suffered hunger and cold before, and knew they could defeat any dangers ahead.

Many were the Chinook People we met. They had endured a hard winter. Food was scarce. One moon must pass before the salmon fish returned. The captains had little to spare and they had many difficulties with these people stealing. One man stole a tomahawk, another lead for bullets, another an ax. Three even stole Seaman.

Pomp burst out, "Did Captain Lewis get him back?"
"Yes, with great difficulty."

When Captain Lewis learned his dog had been stolen, his anger exploded. He sent three men in pursuit with orders to shoot the Chinook if they did not return Seaman. Never before had either captain ordered their men to shoot any of the people we met, for they wished only good relations with them.

While the men were gone, Captain Lewis stormed around like someone possessed by an evil spirit. Everyone stayed away from him, including Captain Clark. By nightfall, the three men returned with Seaman barking and jumping upon Captain Lewis.

This pleased him, but he remained angry and went to the chief, telling him that unless the stealing stopped, he would use his rifles against the Chinook. The chief signed that bad men had caused the trouble. He would tell them to end their thieving, as he wished to be friends with the Americans.

Each night the captains placed guards around our camp.

The captains were eager to reach the Pierced Nose People because travel on the river was too slow. Captain Clark walked ahead to trade for five horses.

Captain Lewis tried to trade for many more horses with the Chinook. He offered our canoes. The Chinook did not want them. Desperate, he pointed to the largest of our kettles. Never before had either captain considered trading a kettle, but Captain Lewis did so now. He got ten horses. With the horses we left the river, but only after Captain Lewis burned all the canoes.

My legs and back ached, for the horses carried our things as we walked. The walking felt good, better than sitting all day in a canoe. You were heavy, Pomp, and wiggled like a worm on a hook. My arms soon tired. York and Colter carried you on their backs. You laughed with the bouncing rides they gave.

The captains needed more horses, but had little left to trade. The Walla Walla People whom we met asked much for their animals. There was a Shoshoni woman living with them. Through her I was able help make the trades.

The chief of the Walla Walla gave Captain Lewis a beautiful white horse, which he greatly desired. In return, the chief wished for one of our four kettles, but the captain would not part with another kettle. He offered his best sword and many bullets and gunpowder. These the chief accepted.

The chief told the captains of a shorter way through the mountains, one which would save many days. The captains were pleased and that night the Americans and Indians celebrated.

Monsieur Cruzatte took his violin out of its leather case and played. First, the Americans danced inside a circle of many Indians. Then the Indians danced as the white men watched. Much to the pleasure of the Indians, the Americans joined their dance. Papa danced with you, toddling in a circle. York, Colter, even Captain Clark, danced with you.

The hard times among the Chinook were put behind us, and Captain Lewis smiled again.

We soon met with the Pierced Nose People. The captains had little left to trade for food, but I helped Captain Clark doctor the sick among them. When we had been with the Pierced Nose People, Captain Clark had healed an old man's leg. The man was very grateful. He was pleased to see Captain Clark again and had told his band of the captain's healing powers. Captain Clark treated sore eyes, aching arms, and injured legs. The people paid him in dogs, roots, and horses.

Soon we saw the Shining Mountains once more. Winter snows lay deep upon the peaks. The chiefs said three weeks must pass before the snows would melt enough for us to cross.

No one looked forward to crossing them again, but we must.

Twisted Hair, a chief of the Pierced Nose People, returned our horses, which he had cared for over the winter. The horses had been ill-used and the captains were displeased. The Pierced Nose People had more horses than any tribe we had met, yet they did not care for their horses as the Shoshoni did. Maybe it was because they had such a wealth of horses it made little difference to them how the horses fared.

Twisted Hair had been in an argument with Chief Cut Nose. Many harsh words passed between them. The captains called the chiefs together to make peace. I stood with the captains and through "Returned From a Faraway Country," my Shoshoni friend of the year before, translated their words from Shoshoni into Hidatsa, which Papa said in his tongue and Labiche told to the captains in their tongue.

Captain Lewis talked from the time the sun rose until it stood over our heads. He asked them to seek peace between themselves and the people living east of the mountains, especially the Blackfeet. He told them his great chief Jefferson had more trading goods than could be piled within the circle of their camp and he would fill a house with guns, gunpowder, bullets, blankets, knives, and kettles to trade for their skins and furs. He told them of the strength and power of the United States and asked them to come under the protection of its flag. He wished the chiefs should journey over the mountains with him and go to the home of his chief in Washington where they would be greeted with many presents.

The captain's words calmed the chiefs and peace passed between them.

It was here, Pomp, you became terribly ill. Both Captain Clark and I cared for you.

"What was wrong with me?" Pomp asked.

Your first teeth were coming in and your gums pained you. Your head burned like a hot stone day and night. Your neck became swollen. I gave you willow bark tea. Captain Clark treated you with his medicines and a poultice of hot onions he held to your neck. You cried with pain all through the night. I feared I would lose you. As my mother did when I was with fever, I stroked your hair and bathed your face with cool water until the fever left your body.

Food became scarce. The captains gave each man a few trade goods: paints, ribbons, and awls. They ordered them to make the best trades they could, for each man must obtain his own food to cross the mountains. The captains cut the brass buttons off their coats for trade as did the men. The captains gave Papa goods to trade and he was able to get us roots and fish.

I worried for you, for I remembered the hunger of the first crossing. You were eating meat and roots now, too. I ate little and saved food for you in my parfleche.

The days seemed long while we waited for the snows to melt. To entertain themselves the Americans and the Pierced Nose People held many contests. They raced horses, shot guns, raced on foot, fired arrows at moving targets, and gambled. You watched these things and played with the other children.

And we watched the snow slowly disappear off the mountains until after a moon, we began our journey again.

We had food. We had horses. We had guns and bullets. But I worried. Did we have the strength to cross those bitter mountains again, especially as our friends the Pierced Nose People warned us it was too early to attempt such a crossing?

Captain Lewis was determined to try. Nothing would change his mind.

I hugged you close as we rode off in the early morning rain. Papa and our pack horses trailed behind.

chapter 25

The first day was dangerous. Trees had fallen across the trail and the rain made the rocks slippery. In the open meadows I wished to stop and dig for more camas roots, as they were very plentiful. Their flowers covered fields, which lay like ponds of blue water. Many, too, were the columbine, violets, bluebells, and peas. Captain Lewis refused to stop.

The next day we reached the snows, which lay higher than a man's head. The snow was firm and made good footing for the horses. But the trail was buried and we could not find it. Still Captain Lewis ordered us on.

We had been three days gone when the captains realized travel was impossible. We must have a guide to lead us over the mountains. Two men went back to the Pierced Nose People to hire a guide. Captain Lewis told them to offer three rifles and ten horses to the man who would lead us to the falls of the Missouri. Never before had he offered such wealth.

We could not remain where we were, so the men

built a wooden scaffold upon which we placed our food for crossing the mountains.

With great disappointment we retreated down the slope. I could tell the captains were disappointed. Not once had they retraced their steps before.

We camped where there was grass for the horses and waited for the guide. Instead of one, three came. We again began climbing the mountains. Our guides understood the mountains well. They knew where the trail lay, even under the snow, and where grass grew in snow-free meadows.

The first night our guides made a ceremony to bring fair weather for the crossing. They set fire to many trees, which blazed like huge torches. You stretched out your hands as if to touch them as they flared in the darkness.

The second day we returned to the scaffold, packed the horses, and rode over ridges and into valleys. We reached the place where one river flows west down the mountain and another river flows east on the other side. We crossed in six suns what had taken us eleven the fall before.

To celebrate we stopped at a hot springs. The Indians had dammed it with stones to make a pool in which to bathe. The men sat in the hot water until they could stay no longer, then leaped up and plunged into an icy stream, shouting all the while. When the men finished I bathed you, Pomp. You splashed and played. You cried when I made you get out, for you were as red as a flashing salmon. Never before had you had such a bath.

We rested while the horses fed and regained their strength. The captains decided to split into two groups. Captain Lewis and nine men would travel north to learn the land there. Captain Clark and his group would travel to the River of Yellow Stones. There they would build canoes and float down the river to where it joined the Missouri. We would meet them there in one moon.

I told Captain Clark I knew the way from the Three Forks to the River of Yellow Stones for this was the path The People took to hunt the buffalo. I had traveled it with my family when I was your age. He was puzzled, for he had thought me desiring to return to the Shoshoni. I told him we would not find The People now. It was summer, and they retreated to the mountains to seek protection from their enemies.

This, too, was the route the Hidatsa took when I was captured. I had made pictures in my mind of the trail so I could follow it back to The People when I escaped.

I could save Captain Clark many days of travel if I found the trail. I thought of Old Toby and how he had gotten lost. I prayed to the Great Spirit to show me the way so I could guide the men.

We traveled down the river valleys, crossing and

recrossing the rivers and streams. The water was high and splashed over the backs of the horses. We got wet. Men hunted so we had meat. I dug bitterroots, which I boiled and mashed. These you liked almost as much as you like yampas carrots now.

In one large meadow I signed to Captain Clark I knew this place well. The People often came here to gather roots. I told him there was the trail over the mountains, which would save us many miles to the Three Forks. He asked me to lead the way. I knew the trail well for it was the one The People used to reach this high meadow.

We struggled against the wind until we reached the mountain gap. The wind died and we traveled fast. That night we built great fires to warm ourselves and dry our things. I saw many signs The People had been here recently gathering yampas roots, but we saw none of them. It was as I had feared, that the Shoshoni had fled to the safety of the mountains already that season. It was here you first tasted the yampas carrots, which both you and Captain Clark came to like.

In another day we reached the place where the captains had cached their goods the summer before. I laughed, for as soon as the men recognized the place, many leaped off their horses and began digging up the supplies. I was curious as to what they desired so much and soon learned it was tobacco. The men had none for six moons. Captain Clark divided it, keeping some to share with the men of Captain Lewis. The other things the captains had left were undamaged and this pleased Captain Clark.

The canoes were undamaged, except one, which had a great crack. The men repaired it and prepared the others for the trip down the river.

Captain Clark split the men again. Some took the horses and followed us along the shore while we rode the canoes to the Three Forks.

Many streams, filled with meltwater, joined our river as it tumbled out of the mountains. The river grew wider and deeper and faster. We rounded a bend and saw Beaverhead Rock.

Many deer, elk, and beaver roamed the valleys and the men hunted well. The beaver were so many that the whacking of their tails awakened us at night. The mosquitoes returned to bother us except at night, for then it became quite cool. Your face and hands were swollen from their bites, as we had eaten the last of the bear fat in crossing the mountains.

We came to a place where I told captain Clark we could leave the river and cross the last low mountains by land. I pointed to him a gap in the mountains and told him this was the trail the Hidatsa had followed when they took me to the River of Yellow Stones.

Captain Clark ordered eleven men to take the six canoes and travel down the river to the Missouri. They were to continue on the Missouri to the great falls and there meet Captain Lewis. Then they would come down the Missouri until it joined the River of Yellow Stones and meet us there. I grew with fear, for each time we split apart our strength was smaller and the dangers from the Blackfeet and Hidatsa greater. Captain Clark, understanding this danger, urged the men to hurry as would he with the rest of the men and the horses.

Hurry we did, crossing many miles until we found the buffalo trail leading to the gap I told about. Once across we rode quickly. As streams join rivers to make them larger, so do the buffalo trails join. Here many trails came together to make a very wide trail. This we followed until we reached the banks of the River of Yellow Stones.

One night Crow Indians stole twenty-four horses. Captain Clark ordered four men to take the rest of the horses across country to the Mandan village and sell them.

The rest of the men built a raft, large enough to carry us and our packs. Papa told Captain Clark he had seen Indians watching us from the rocks. We frequently saw signals of smoke rising. This meant our enemies knew of our presence. Hurry, I urged the men, for I did not wish to be captured ever again.

The men did, and soon we floated upon the river. We kept well to the river's center during the day and stopped on islands at night. One afternoon we saw a great rock rising above the flat plains. We stopped to rest. We climbed the rock with Captain Clark. On the top were two stone piles placed there by Indians. Many pictures of buffalo, elk, and beaver they had painted on the rock. With his knife Captain Clark carved his name into the rock. He held you up and turned you in the four directions in the Shoshoni way and gave this rock a special name.

"Do you know what it is?"

"Pompy's Rock," Pomp said proudly.

"Yes."

We reached the end of the River of Yellow Stones in a few suns. The only dangers we met were many white bears. Even in our canoes they threatened us, plunging into the water and swimming after us until the men fired upon them. One almost reached us before a spray of bullets stopped him.

"But why were the bears chasing you?" Pomp asked.

"Either they were angered when we disturbed them or because we had meat with us and they hungered for it."

We camped where we camped the year before. And, as before, game was scarce and mosquitoes many. Captain Clark was surprised when the men with horses appeared only four days behind us. They were without the horses and riding in two bullboats, made in the Mandan way. They told him the Crow had stolen the rest of the horses, so they killed two bull buffaloes, skinned them, and made their boats.

I was pleased, for now we were stronger.

We were to wait for Captain Lewis at the mouth of the River of Yellow Stones. But after several days Captain Clark grew impatient with the lack of meat and the fierce mosquitoes. The mosquitoes were so many the men could not even aim their rifles, for they blocked the sights. Captain Clark wrote a piece of paper for Captain Lewis, stuck it on a pole, and we set off down the river to wait for him at a more suitable site.

We went slowly, giving Captain Lewis time to catch us. I worried for Captain Lewis, as he had been gone over a moon from us. Yet Captain Clark did not seem to worry, so great was his faith in his friend.

One afternoon we met two white men in a canoe coming up the river just as we had done a year before. They told Captain Clark many things. The captain was disappointed to learn their efforts to make peace among the tribes had failed. The Minnetree and Mandan were attacking the Arikara. The Sioux were fighting all they encountered.

Captain Clark decided we must wait until Captain Lewis joined us. To enter hostile lands with so few men would be foolish. We made camp, dried our things, and I dug many roots.

We did not have to wait long. The next day, five canoes rounded a great bend and shouting arose from our men and the men of Captain Lewis. The meeting was not a happy one, however, for Captain Lewis had been gravely wounded in an accident. It appears that Monsieur Cruzatte, whose fingers were so skillful on the strings of the violin, was not very skillful on a rifle. Thinking he was shooting an elk, he shot Captain Lewis in the rump. The wound was deep. The bullet had passed through and was very painful. Captain Lewis was forced to lie on his stomach, the pain was so horrible.

Captain Clark immediately attended to his wound, cleaning it and treating it with his many medicines. As he did so, he told Captain Lewis of our journey and of the loss of the horses. Captain Lewis shared his tale of danger and disappointment. He had traveled to the great falls. In stopping some Blackfeet warriors from stealing guns, one warrior had been killed. Now he feared warfare with the Blackfeet.

In the morning the raft and the canoes were loaded again. As we floated down the river, I wondered what lay ahead for us. Would the Mandan still be friendly to the captains? Would Papa wish to remain with the Mandan? Would Otter Woman rejoin us?

In four swift days, we reached the village of the Mandan.

Great was the celebration that night. Monsieur Cruzatte played until his fingers could no longer dance upon the strings. Meat was shared and the captains traded many elk and buffalo skins for maize.

My heart soared when I saw Otter Woman. She hugged me and held you and we talked and laughed long into the night. She had feared we would never return.

Captain Clark talked long with the chiefs One Eye, Black Cat, and Big White. They told him of the fights between tribes, and he urged them to find peace. He asked the chiefs to travel with him to meet his chief Jefferson. All while Captain Clark talked, Captain Lewis lay on his stomach, too weak to participate in the council.

Captain Clark talked to Papa, asking him to come to Saint Louis to interpret again, for Papa spoke the Minnetree tongue and one of their chiefs would travel with the captains.

I was excited. I did not wish to leave the company

of the captains. We had journeyed much time and very far together. I had seen many wonders and now wished to see the great village of Saint Louis.

Papa was eager to go, too, for his work with the captains would continue.

Unfortunately, the attacks of the Sioux along the river frightened the Minnetree chief from going with the captains. Captain Clark told Papa now his work with them was finished. Captain Clark called Papa his friend and Papa beamed with pleasure. Captain Clark paid Papa many dollars for our tipi, his horse, and for his efforts on the journey.

Captain Clark asked Papa if you could go with him to Saint Louis, where he would raise you as his son. He would teach you the ways of the white men, and you would be wise in the eyes of your people.

No, not yet, I said to Papa and Captain Clark. You were too young, but someday you would make this journey, just as you had traveled to where the land ends in the great waters of the ocean.

Early in the morning the captains and their men pointed their canoes downstream. We stood on the bank as the current grabbed them and pulled them away.

I held you tight, too tight, for you whimpered. My heart ached. I would miss them. I would miss York with his strong hands and gentle fingers. Cruzatte's music would fade from my memory. Seaman's eager bark would be but an echo in my heart. Captain Lewis's stern, determined look would remain, however, but I would miss his great curiosity. Most of all I would miss Captain Clark and how his eyes danced when he held you. Never would I forget his many kindnesses to you and me.

I closed my eyes, for tears ran.

Would we ever see the captains again? I wondered.

Where would their life circles turn?

I wished to stay and I wished to go. How could a heart be torn in two directions?

I opened my eyes as the canoes disappeared around a bend. Captain Clark's fiery red hair rippled in the wind, waving farewell.

"Saint Louis!" Papa shouted. "Look, Jean Baptiste," he cried. "We are there."

Pomp sprang up and dashed to his father's side.

Slowly, Sacagawea stood and joined her family.

She scanned the shore for hair of fire. She did not see it. A sadness entered her.

Then Captain Clark lifted his cap and waved it in greeting. Warmth flooded her heart.

Is this where my journey ends? Sacagawea wondered.

Authors' Note

Sacagawea is one of the best known women in American history. She has been honored more than any other woman in our history. Mountains, rivers, lakes, and parks are named Sacagawea. Across the country there are monuments and memorials dedicated to her. Sacagawea's unique contributions to the success of the Lewis and Clark expedition are being honored through her image on the new dollar coin to be minted in the year 2000.

Her role in aiding the Lewis and Clark expedition places her in the forefront of our American story.

But who was Sacagawea? Was she solely a guide for Lewis and Clark? Or did she help the expedition in moments of crisis? Who was she as a person? As a mother? As a Shoshoni girl living far from her beloved Shining Mountains?

To find the answers to these questions we imaginatively journeyed with Sacagawea. Using the journals of Lewis and Clark as our guide, we walked in her footsteps as she carried her infant son, Pomp. We sat with her in a canoe as she fought mosquitoes. We wondered with her at the world beyond the Shining Mountains. We braved the western wilderness and weather with her as she crossed half of the continent.

Sacagawea's story and life began sometime before 1790 in the Shining Mountains, known today as the Rockies. No one is certain of her birth date, but she was born into a nomadic band of Shoshoni Indians.

Sacagawea's life until her capture by her tribe's enemies, the Hidatsa, was typical of Shoshoni life. She traveled with her family as they moved from summer to winter camps following seasonal plants and animals. She played with her friends, gathered foods, cooked, sewed, and mastered the many tasks a Shoshoni woman needed to know.

Around 1800, Sacagawea was captured by the Hidatsa and forced into slavery. She was taken from her beloved Shining Mountains to the plains of North Dakota, where she encountered an entirely new way of life. It was while living with the Hidatsa that Sacagawea became the wife of the French interpreter and trader Toussaint Charbonneau. He apparently won her as payment for a gambling debt. They lived with the Mandan Indians along the Missouri near present-day Bismarck, North Dakota.

In the fall of 1804, the Lewis and Clark expedition reached the Mandan village, the first major stop on their way west to the Pacific Ocean. The expedition built winter quarters nearby and prepared to continue their journey across North America.

Lewis and Clark hired Charbonneau as an interpreter for the expedition, as he spoke several Indian languages and was familiar with the tribes along the Missouri. Lewis and Clark were eager to have Sacagawea, although pregnant, join them, for she spoke Shoshoni. The captains were determined to trade with Shoshoni for the horses they desperately needed to cross the Rockies.

Before the Corps of Discovery proceeded in the spring of 1805, Sacagawea gave birth to her son, Jean Baptiste Charbonneau, called "Pomp" by the Americans.

With her skills as a food gatherer, her knowledge of plants and animals, her courage, her hardiness, and her steadfastness, Sacagawea became an integral part of the expedition. Several times she saved precious materials from loss, found much-needed food, and guided the Corps where she knew the land. All the while she cared for and nourished Pomp as she carried him across the continent.

As he had promised, Captain Clark educated Pomp in St. Louis from the time he was about six years old. Pomp later traveled to Europe before returning to the West, where he lived his life as a guide, interpreter, trapper, and trader until he died in 1866.

Sacagawea apparently died on December 29, 1812, at Fort Manuel along the Missouri River. It is recorded there, "This evening the wife of Charbonneau, a Snake (Shoshoni) squaw, died of putrid fever. She was a good and the best woman in the fort, aged about 25 years. She left a fine infant girl." History does not record much more about her daughter, Lizette.

Another version of Sacagawea's death claims she died on the Wind River Shoshoni Reservation in 1884.

This book was inspired when we heard author Stephen Ambrose describe Sacagawea's role in the success of the Lewis and Clark expedition. His image of Sacagawea traveling with her small family in the vastness of the West with men far from their friends and relatives remained with us until we could write Sacagawea's story through her own eyes. To Stephen we say, "Thank you!"

Research for this book was conducted at the Western Expansion National Park in St. Louis, at Lewis and Clark sites along their trail from Missouri to Oregon, at the Mandan Village in North Dakota, at the North Dakota Lewis and Clark Interpretive Center, at Fort Clatsop in Oregon, and at the most beautiful campsites in America along the upper Missouri, places where, so long ago, Sacagawea also camped.

Historical Note

In 1803, France sold the Louisiana Territory to the United States for $15 million. This land purchase doubled the size of the young United States. This vast new territory, known by Native Americans but unknown by Americans, intrigued President Thomas Jefferson. He was determined to learn about the land, peoples, plants, and animals of this new addition to the United States. Thus was born the Lewis and Clark expedition.

President Jefferson gave Captain Meriwether Lewis orders to create the Corps of Discovery. Lewis chose his friend William Clark to help him lead the Corps. They selected twenty-nine brave young men to form the Corps. Their mission: explore the Missouri River, cross the Rocky Mountains, and travel to the Pacific Ocean, all the while searching for a water route across North America.

In May 1804, the Lewis and Clark expedition began its two-and-a-half-year-long journey across and into the pages of history. The Corps was frequently aided by Native Americans. Without the knowledge of the plants, animals, and terrain that the native peoples provided, along with food, the expedition might never have succeeded.

Critical to this success was the expedition's meeting with the Shoshoni. They had the horses the Corps needed to cross the towering Rocky Mountains. There, back home in her beloved Shining Mountains, Sacagawea played one of her most valuable roles.

In February 1805, Sacagawea joined the Corps for this express purpose: to aid in obtaining the necessary horses. Yet, while carrying and caring for her infant son, Pomp, she also helped the Corps in many untold ways, from finding much-needed food to guiding the Corps through unknown lands.

When the Corps returned to St. Louis in September 1806, they were welcomed as returning heroes. Many Americans had given them up for lost. However, through all the toil and hardships the expedition encountered, only one man died (apparently from appendicitis).

With the knowledge and experience Lewis and Clark gained, the United States was prepared to grow beyond the Mississippi River and reach for the Pacific.